MW00987904

GUNNAR

MAMMOTH FOREST WOLVES - BOOK THREE

KIMBER WHITE

NOKAY PRESS LLC

For all the latest on my new releases and exclusive content, sign up for my newsletter. http://bit.ly/241WcfX

ONE

GUNNAR

Pain is a symphony. Each movement blends and crescendos until you are swept away to another time, another place, another being. You cannot control it. You cannot bend it. You can only let it take you. That is the secret. You must let it happen to you. Give over to it. It will win every time.

Today, my tormentor was the maestro. Each punishing blow to my core took away pieces of me. Had he just stayed with that, I might have been able to stay on my feet. He didn't though. Maestro studied every ragged breath I took. I couldn't see him. Part of his genius was to keep me blindfolded. I had never once seen his face. But, I could scent him a mile away. He smelled of musk and pine. I could sense his movements from the change in the air. I tried to brace for the next kick. I shouldn't have done that. I forgot the first lesson. I tried to control it. The next kick hit me in the back where I didn't expect it.

Mercifully, blackness came for me. He'd gone too far.

Later, sunlight hit my cheek. I lay in something wet and sticky. The urge to cough gripped me and I spread my palms on the ground, trying to stop it. My ribs were broken again. They would heal in a few hours if they left me alone. I tried to open my eyes, but once again they were swollen shut.

"Gunnar!" A hushed whisper reached my ears. It hurt to try and listen. God, had they ruptured my eardrum this time?

I got one eye open and saw the hand crawling toward me. It seemed odd, almost disembodied, the bent fingers skittering toward me like a spider. He touched my wrist and feeling returned to my body in wave after wave of agony. I exhaled, trying not to bend to it.

"You in there?" the voice reached me again.

I couldn't hold the coughing fit back. It wracked through my broken body, waking me fully.

"Yeah," I managed to choke out. I spat blood from my mouth and tried to sit upright. Big mistake. The room spun. I slid backward, propping my back against the wall. Calling it a room was a stretch. This was little more than a cage. Four cement walls boxing an eight-foot by eight-foot patch of straw-covered ground. The roof was thatched grass and straw, not sturdy enough to keep the rain out.

One huff and puff from this big bad wolf and I could have blown the place to smithereens. Except for one thing.

Dragonsteel.

They'd chained my wrists and ankles with it, anchoring me to a post somewhere outside the cell. Even at full strength, I couldn't break through it. Dragonsteel is the only metal strong enough to hold back a shifter like me.

"Gunnar!" The voice reached me again. Each syllable of my name scraped against my consciousness, like the worst hangover you can possibly imagine.

"I'm awake," I whispered back. "Relax, Finn. They haven't killed me...yet."

Finn's soft laughter grated too. He gave me a thumbs up through the gap in the wall between our cells. He withdrew his hand and I heard shuffling straw as Finn crawled to the other side of his cell. The air seemed to shift as Finn set off a series of signals starting with the cell on the other side of his. More shuffling, a cough here and there as the rest of the inmates got word I'd survived another day.

Every day was like this. Sometimes my captors came for me in the middle of the night, sometimes first thing in the morning. Sometimes they kept me for days. Each time, the rest of the inmates at Camp Hell would wait for me to return, each time certain that I wouldn't.

"No one's survived as long as you have, Gunnar," Finn told me after my first week here. It was a dubious honor, but I supposed I had to take good news where I could.

"Glad to have you back," Finn said. Just the tips of his fingers appeared through the gap in the wall. I pushed through the agony and reached over to put my palm over them. Finn's flesh burned hot. He was a wolf shifter like me, so that alone wasn't cause for alarm. But, in Finn's case it felt like a true fever.

Finn had been in Camp Hell longer than any of us. At least, that's what he told me. He was here when I got here. Others I'd heard were carried out in the middle of the night. New prisoners came in to fill their spots. Finn had been the lone holdout next to me.

I used to scratch the passing days in the dirt where it stayed the driest. I made it all the way to one hundred. Then, I stopped. It might be two hundred days now. It felt like more.

"Was it Maestro?" Finn asked.

"Yes." I drew my knees up, wincing past the pain in my ribs. The skin stretched taut around them and started to itch. Molly would tell me that was a good sign. I was healing.

Molly. If I closed my eyes, I could see her. Her features were no longer vivid in my mind's eye though. I could see her wide, brown eyes, her dark hair with thick bangs cut straight across. She had an infectious, deep laugh. Molly was Liam's wife. Studying to become a veterinarian, she took care of the wounded in Mammoth Forest. That kept her ever busier.

Pressing the back of my head against the cement wall, I tried to imagine the caves beneath Mammoth Forest where we hid from the Pack. It was dangerous to do so. It's what Maestro and the Chief Pack wanted from me. It was the only reason I was still alive.

Months ago...hell...for all I knew it could have been years...I had been captured by the Pack trying to rescue the women they meant to enslave. Would I do it again? I knew I would. They were innocent, human. If I'd done nothing, those women would have been marked against their will at the Chief Alpha's whim.

They were free now. At least, I hoped to God they were. I saw Mac and Payne spiriting them away just before the Pack closed in. As I squeezed my eyes shut, that scene played out in my mind a thousand times. Mac shouting. Payne taking a hit. Dozens of girls busting through the wrought iron gates surrounding Birch Haven College. The brochure called it paradise; in reality it was another form of prison.

Had I imagined it? Had the whole thing just been a trick of my mind to make me think all this was worth it? I suffered, but the people I cared most about got away. I'd done my duty.

"Don't fall asleep on me, man," Finn said. He smacked his palm against the ground. Finn's knuckles were gnarled. Three of his fingernails had been torn away, leaving puckered flesh behind. He wasn't an Alpha wolf like I was. It took him longer to heal and when he did, his scars were probably worse.

"I'm awake," I said, coughing up blood.

"Good. What do you want me to tell Rackham and Jones?"

Rackham had the cell on the other side of Finn. Jones was on Rackham's other side. Sometimes, I could hear Rackham moaning in his sleep. I'd never heard Jones at all. He could be a figment of Rackham's imagination for all I knew. Finn said Rackham was a beta wolf like him. I got the impression they'd known each other on the outside, though Finn would never say anything like that for sure. None of us would. The Pack could be listening. It was also entirely possible that Finn himself was a member of the Pack put here to ferret information from me.

I kept my guard up. So did Finn. And yet, Finn knew who I was. Somehow, he'd managed to see me dragged in. I didn't have to say a word. The ink on my chest would have told him everything he needed to know.

The tattoo had been Jagger Wilkes's idea. Years ago, he'd been the first of us to break free from the Pack's influence. His cousin Liam had gone with him. They brought Mac along. Then, they found me. The moment we left the Pack, we were hunted traitors. Rebels. Resistance fighters, though that was never what we set out to be. At first, we just wanted to get away.

But, with freedom comes great responsibility. We couldn't stand by and watch the horrors of the Pack unfold. We found hidden caves in Mammoth Forest. We set up camp. Then slowly, year after year, we helped others get out too. To prove our loyalty to each other and our cause, Liam, Mac, Jagger and I marked ourselves. The sprawling tattoo now took up the upper part of my chest. A black wolf's head with great, unfurled wings, and beneath that, two crossed daggers. The Pack knows anyone bearing this mark is a traitor. It seemed like a good idea at the time. Now, it made them want to hurt me worse.

"Tell them whatever you want," I said. It got hard to hold my head up. Finn might raise holy hell, but I damn well wanted to sleep. One of the guards could come back at any moment. Or, they might not come back for days.

"Hang in there, man," Finn said. He always said it. In the past, it had given me comfort. Now, I just wanted to be left alone.

"I'm all right," I said, sliding my hand beneath the gap in the wall. "I'm just going to rest a little while. Is it dawn or evening?"

Finn's soft laughter gave me a small amount of comfort. "Evening," he said. "You missed dinner. Gray slop."

I switched positions, putting my weight on my left hip. Slowly, I lowered myself to the ground and kicked the chains out from underneath me. I would give anything to shift into my wolf. In the beginning, the urge to let him out nearly drove me mad. As the weeks wore on, I felt him go quiet. The chains kept my inner wolf at bay as well. Fucking dragonsteel. How the hell the Pack managed to get their hands on so much of it was another great mystery.

"I'm going to go to sleep now, Finn," I said. "That's the way it's gonna be. Don't worry. You'll hear me breathing. I hope."

Finn let out a little growl. I couldn't bear to think how long he'd had to contain his own wolf. He was still alive though. His mind still mostly sound. Was it easier for betas? I had to think it was. Morbid as it was, Finn was the canary in the coal mine for me. As long as he was here, I wasn't done yet either.

I laid my cheek against my hand. My chest pulled tight as I put weight on my side. But slowly, carefully, I let myself go. The cell spun and my stomach rolled, but I kept my breathing steady.

Finn started to hum. He'd do it whenever I stopped talking to him. I used to hate it; now it gave me a strange comfort.

A full moon rose. Its bright halo seemed to waver as I watched it through the tiny slits in the thatched roof. It seemed so close, as if I could reach out and touch it.

Finn went silent except for his slow, ragged breaths. His fingers beneath the wall went slack and finally withdrew as he must have rolled to his other side. There was nothing more to listen to beyond my own heartbeat.

I don't know how long I lay there. Long enough that my ribs reknit. An hour? Maybe two. Clouds rolled in to block the moon. I couldn't hear Finn breathing anymore. My heart thundered inside of me. No. Not tonight.

The shock of silence made me sit straight up. I bit past the searing pain in my side. I would have called to him. I would have rattled the chains as loud as I could. But there was something out there. Something that made every other creature in the woods dart for cover.

I crouched as low as I could, trying to see through the gap in the wall to the woods beyond.

A pair of dark eyes appeared through the bushes. My heart

went still. I couldn't move. I couldn't breathe. Heat snaked its way through my chest and my vision wavered. Hot breath caressed my cheek. The eyes blinked once. Twice.

She.

The truth of it slammed into my chest with as much force as any of Maestro's blows. There was a woman out there. Her scent poured over me, warm, sweet and strong. I dug my fingers into the ground. My inner wolf stirred with more force than I'd felt in weeks. With no conscious thought, a growl ripped from me.

I felt her heart trip. I'd scared her. Acting on instinct, I launched myself toward the gap in the wall. I had to get out. I had to see her. Branches cracked and the bushes shimmied. Then, the pair of brown eyes disappeared. She was gone.

"The fuck are you doing, Gunnar?" Finn shouted. Beside him, Rackham stirred. I could hear his own chains rattle. My wolf had disturbed all of them. They heard my growl.

Stupid. So stupid. The Pack would sense it too.

"Nothing," I said, settling back against the wall. "I just thought I saw something."

"What?"

I didn't mean to give voice to it. But, I did. "A girl," I answered.

Silence, then Finn's deep laugh split the air. "Shit, Gunnar. You had me scared there for a second. I thought you were dying. Relax, Rackham. Gunnar just had himself a wet dream."

"Fuck you," I muttered, drawing my knees to my chest. That got easier too. But, as I did it, I felt a dull, heated throbbing between my legs. Finn was half right. The woman's scent stirred something else inside of me besides my wolf. God, how long had I been in this hellhole? How much longer could I survive?

"Break time's over!" A voice cut through the stillness. Finn's chains rattled as he moved to the far corner of his cell.

The clouds lifted and the full moon shone bright. Leaves crunched under heavy, booted footsteps.

Maestro was back.

TWO

JETT

He was fast. But, I was stealthy. I heard him before I saw him. He wasn't where he was supposed to be. The evening patrols usually stayed to the northeast until after midnight. This guy had either gotten lax, or maybe they'd issued new orders. In any event, the ground crunched beneath his feet as I hid behind the brush. I just managed to dive through the tunnel opening before he got to me.

I didn't move, not even to breathe. Just a thin layer of foliage and bundled branches stood between me and disaster. Leaves crunched under his heavy footsteps. He stopped just a few feet from the camouflaged trap door. Earth rained down over my face as he drew closer. The moon was too bright. If he looked down...hell...if the wind changed, he'd find me.

A shout from the camp drew his attention and my heart started to beat again.

"Murphy! You're gonna need to help me get him out. His legs are gone."

"Son of a bitch," Murphy muttered. "If they ended up killing that fucker, I am not taking the heat for it."

I started to breathe easier as Murphy turned toward camp. From my vantage point, he looked giant. I stared straight up his tree trunk legs. He had a mass of thick black hair hanging past his shoulders. Running a hand over the rough stubble on his chin, he cocked his head and started to walk back. I got brave, straightening. I threaded my fingers through the tangled tree roots we'd tied to the makeshift door. Murphy froze. The wind changed. His nostrils flared and he turned back toward the woods. I caught a glimpse of his wolf eyes flashing gold beneath the moonlight. That was a good sign. If his eyes went blood-red, I'd be in deep shit.

Finally, he turned his back to me and headed the other way. I squeezed the tree branches so hard I'm surprised they didn't turn to powder. I waited, watching Murphy's back as he trudged through the thick brush and out of sight. Slowly, I emerged from my hole in the ground.

I couldn't risk standing upright. All it would take was one careless step and Murphy or one of the others would catch my scent. The smartest play would have been staying hidden in the tunnel. No, the even smarter play would have been to get the hell out of here or never come in the first place. Vera's stern voice rose up in my mind. If she knew I came out here tonight, I wouldn't put it past her to seal up the tunnels behind me.

Carefully picking my way through the brush, I got the camp in my line of sight again. Raising my scope to my eye, I zeroed in on the cinderblock cells. I counted five of them in this quadrant.

To the east, there were ten more. Those were empty though. I'd been there last night.

I couldn't be sure, but my guess was only four of those cells had current occupants. The walls didn't go all the way to the ground, leaving about a half a foot gap in each. It was how the guards passed food to the inmates. When I pressed my cheek to the ground, I could see legs and feet in three of them. The last cell on the easternmost side drew my attention. Its occupant was lying on his side, his face pointed toward the opening.

My breath caught as I focused my scope straight at him. The moon shone bright enough that I could make out his features. Hell, if I wanted to, if I had the laser sight, I probably could have gotten a shot off. Maybe that would have been for the best. A bullet straight between the eyes might be something he'd beg for if he knew it was an option.

My heart thundered in my chest as I watched him sleep. A week's worth of grime covered his face. His hair might have been blond, but it was matted with dirt and blood. He had a deep gash over his right eye. On a normal man, it might have been a mortal wound. On a wolf shifter like him, he'd probably heal by morning.

He was big. Huge, actually. Even lying down, his long legs stretched almost to the opposite side of the cell. How tall would that make him, I wondered. Six and a half feet, at least. Though his face looked gaunt from malnutrition, he had striking, broad cheekbones and a generous mouth. It curved up as he slept as if he were dreaming of something pleasant. I found myself hoping he was. Poor fucker. It was probably the only time he ever got peace. Yes. A quick bullet in the brain from *my* rifle would bring him mercy he probably didn't deserve. He was still a shifter, after all.

His eyes snapped open and my world seemed to shift on its axis. In a tiny instant, he found my gaze. His eyes went from cold blue to glinting silver as his wolf stirred.

"Shit," I muttered, crawling backward, commando-style.

He lifted his head. Agony etched deep lines in his brow. He tried to sit up, but his legs didn't seem to work right.

"Gunnar!" A whisper cut through the stillness. "They're back for you!"

He looked straight at me. There could be no doubt. I crouched about fifteen yards away, but he saw me. His agonized expression turned to solemn acceptance as two pairs of booted feet entered his cell. He groaned as arms reached down. The chains binding his wrists and ankles scraped against the ground as they hauled him to his feet. He didn't scream. He didn't beg. He just put one bloodied foot in front of the other as they led him out into the night.

Sweat trickled down my back as I held the rifle steady. I could have ended it. One breath. One beat. One squeeze of the trigger and I could have put the man out of his misery. What then? The guards would have easily tracked where the shot came from. I had the advantage of surprise, but two full-blooded shifters on my scent and I wouldn't make it ten feet.

I should have gone. I'd seen enough, hadn't I? I promised Melanie I'd only wanted to see if any new prisoners had been brought in since the last time we ran recon. Now I knew. They had. It didn't prove anything conclusive, of course, but it was a lead. We'd heard rumors Birch Haven College had been liberated last year. We heard they'd captured one of the resistance fighters who'd been responsible. If that were true...if this man had been there the day the college had been set free, I had to talk to him. I had to know what happened.

I took to the shadows again, slinging my rifle over my shoulder. It should be safe now for a while. The patrols had passed. This part of the woods would stay quiet for at least an hour. Plenty of time for me to dive back into the tunnels and head back home. I could even be back before Vera and the others woke. Melanie would know where I'd gone, of course. For now, she covered for me with Vera. But, the day would come when we'd have to have a serious conversation.

I leaned against a tall oak tree, letting the rough bark scrape my back. Once, a long time ago, I'd heard these woods had been teeming with Pack members. No one knew why they'd mostly cleared out. Maybe it was so the Alpha could keep the regular members of the Pack from seeing what went on here. This wasn't a normal prison camp, if there was such a thing. Only the worst of the worst were sent here to die.

Gunnar. Was that his name? His cellmate had shouted out a warning. Even now, I could still see the shadow of the other man's legs. He'd fallen asleep himself. The cellblocks were laid out in a straight row. On the other side of him, I saw two more sets of feet. The man on the far end, second from the last, wasn't moving. Come to think of it, I hadn't seen him move at all since I started watching. Dread skittered up my spine. If he was already dead, why did they leave him in there like that?

My heart stopped as I heard the crunch of bone and grunts of pain toward the center of the compound. Gunnar. Could he be the one?

I don't know what compelled me to stay there that night. But, the man was going to die; of that I was sure. I had hoped to go back and tell the others what I saw so we could make a plan together. I knew now with stone-cold certainty that I might not get another chance. Strong as he looked, that shifter might not survive the night.

They kept him for twenty minutes. Twenty minutes. Such a short amount of time, but it had to have seemed an eternity to him. His cell door opened with a clang. Chains scraped against the ground as they threw him back in and shut the door. I flattened myself to the ground so I could see through the six-inch gap in the wall.

Gunnar's face had changed shape. He seemed caught between man and wolf. His nose was broken and his lip split. He let out a great, heaving sigh. I watched his chest rise and fall with his erratic breaths that rattled.

Shit. He was dying. I knew that sound.

I don't remember moving. Before I knew what was happening, I'd crawled on my elbows to within five feet of Gunnar's cell. God. It was even worse up close. They'd caved his chest in. The fingers on his right hand bent back at wrong angles. As I watched, the skin rippled as his body tried to heal.

Don't die. I said it over and over again in my mind. Don't die until I have a chance to find out for sure.

I edged closer, crawling on my belly. I shut my eyes and stopped breathing. I was no shifter. I couldn't sense the Pack. But, I could hear if they were on the move.

Gunnar's eyes snapped open, flashing silver and widening. I froze. As he tried to focus, his smile took on a dream-like quality. He probably didn't know what was real. It felt like *I* didn't.

Then, reality slammed straight into me as his fingers closed around my wrist. Even in his weakened state, he moved faster than I could see. His grip tightened, cutting off the blood flow to my fingers. I couldn't move. I couldn't breathe. All I could do was stare into those piercing silver eyes.

When his fangs came out, I tried not to scream.

THREE

GUNNAR

I tried to die. This time, it felt so close. I floated away, carried on a cloud. That should have been my first clue it wasn't real. If it were that easy, everyone in this place would have gladly gone.

Heat slammed into my chest along with heart-pounding desire. Every sense came sharply into focus. The sky was no longer black; I could see the blue bands of light even in the middle of the night. Her sweet, intoxicating scent wrapped around me, warming my cold places, easing my pain.

Her.

My eyes burst open, my vision tunneled to a single pinpoint of light. When it expanded, sable eyes stared back at me. Her breath brushed my cheek. My inner wolf sprang awake. The urge to shift bubbled from my core.

Mine. Mine. Mine!

I rolled to my belly and pushed myself to the opening at the bottom of the wall. I couldn't see all of her. She strained against me. It was only then I realized I had a hold of her. Delicate bones, smooth, pale skin, a flash of metal.

"Who are you?" My voice ripped from my ragged throat.

She shook her head. Digging her heels into the dirt, she tried to loosen my grip on her wrist. Instinct told me to let go. I wouldn't hurt her. I would never hurt her. But, she was terrified.

"Let go of me," she whispered.

God. Her voice was raspy, dark and sultry. I shivered with desire.

"Who are you?" I said again. She moved. She stopped trying to pull away and crouched low, almost lying on her belly like I was. From this vantage point, I could see all of her. She had a mass of thick, dark hair, deepest brown, or maybe even black. Her brown eyes blinked with a mixture of fear and curiosity. With the pad of my thumb, I felt the frenetic pulse in her wrist.

I didn't mean to do it. Until that moment, I never realized I could. But, I closed my eyes, took a breath and slowed my own pulse. Two beats. Three. Then her pulse slowed to match mine. It was then she started pulling away again.

"Tell me who *you* are!" she demanded. She had all the fire and fury in those dark eyes. It stirred my blood, reawakening the pain from Maestro's last visit. I didn't care. At that moment, I might have endured it all again just for a few more minutes with her.

"Gunnar," I said simply. "Gunnar Cole. Your turn."

Again she shook her head no. "Let me go. I have to go. The patrols are coming back."

My heart jumped. As much as I wanted to keep touching her, the thought of the Pack patrols getting anywhere near her sent ice shooting through my veins. No. I'd die before I let them hurt her. Fuck. I'd die anyway. Trapped in pain and dragonsteel, what the hell could I do about any of it?

The answer slammed into me. I could let her go. I loosened my grip. She slid her wrist out of my fingers.

She didn't run. At first, she didn't even move. She just kept staring at me with those beautiful, inquisitive brown eyes. Whatever effect her touch had on me, she seemed similarly stunned by it.

I sensed the others before she did. "Go!" I whispered. "They can't find you!"

She stayed frozen to her spot, her eyes flicking over me.

Dammit. "Who are you?" I asked for the third time.

Finally, she blinked and started to crawl backward. More than anything, I wanted to tell her to wait. I wanted to touch her again. "Dammit," I yelled in the loudest whisper I dared. "Tell me who the hell you are."

She stopped and tilted her head so she could see me through the gap again. "I can't do that," she answered. "Just...don't die yet, Gunnar Cole."

Voices rose to the east as the Pack patrols drew near. The girl vaulted to her feet. She wore black combat boots covered in dirt. She had a rifle slung across her back. It jostled as she broke into a run.

The Pack was close. I didn't know who the hell she was, but she was just human. If the wolves scented her, they'd be on her in seconds. I gathered my leg chains. They might kill me, but if I could distract the patrol away from her, it might be all the time she needed. Would I do it? Would I risk another beating for a woman who wouldn't even tell me her name?

I never had to make the choice. The impossible happened right before my eyes. Five seconds before the Pack patrols would have had her in their line of sight, the girl dropped straight through the ground and disappeared.

It was a trick of the light or my battered brain. It had to be. Human girls couldn't just vanish into thin air.

Tonight's patrol consisted of three Pack members. I didn't know their names but recognized their scents. They joked and laughed as their heavy boots trudged over the ground a few feet from the cells. One of them stopped right in front of Finn's cell, turned toward it and took a piss.

Finn growled. I put a hand under the wall, gripping the ground. Keep still, I wanted to shout. There was no point riling any of them tonight. I, for one, didn't know if I could survive it. Up until ten minutes ago, that wouldn't have mattered. Now though, the girl's scent still hung in the air, a lingering echo that sent that same shiver of desire through me.

Mine.

The guards moved on. Finn's chains rattled as he scooted closer to the wall. "Fucking Pack sheep," he said. "Without these chains I'd lay all three of them out."

"Sure you would," I said, smiling. "But they're not worth the trouble."

"You still breathing, man?" Finn asked. His hand came under the wall and he pumped his fist against the ground.

"Still doing my thing," I said. I coiled into myself to stave off the round of coughs I felt coming. If I gave in to it, I was sure my ribs would break again.

"We were worried," Finn said. "Maestro hasn't pulled that shit for a while. I don't like it. Something's coming."

I pressed my head against the cement wall. "Something's always coming."

"No, not like this. Jones heard 'em talking after they pulled you out. You notice Maestro's the only one working us over lately? When's the last time anyone's seen Buzzy or Legs?"

Pack interrogators got their names from whatever particular torture preferences were. Buzzy became Buzzy on account of the way most of us felt when he was done with us. Legs was more obvious. He liked to break them.

"I don't know," I answered, defeated. I couldn't think about any of that now. I could only think about the girl. But, Finn said nothing about her.

"Well, Rackham said Jones thinks they're scared. The Alpha's pissed because the others weren't getting any results."

"Results?"

Finn went quiet. That alone would have given me pause. His incessant chatter gave me comfort most nights. After a full minute went by without his answer, I leaned closer to the wall between us.

"Finn! What are you talking about?"

Finn let out a sigh. "You, Gunnar. Rackham says Jones heard them say you've held out longer than anybody ever has."

"Lucky me. Does that mean I get a medal?"

"Don't joke. You know exactly what it means. Rackham says Jones heard them talking about the Alpha coming down here himself. Maybe as early as next week."

My heart went stone cold. If the Alpha were indeed coming to Camp Hell, it could only mean one thing. Subjugation.

The Chief Pack's Alpha exerted total control over members of his pack. They worked like spokes on a wheel with him at the hub. He controlled his top, most trusted generals to keep his territories under control. The pull of the Pack was the thing everyone here feared. It's what I, Jagger, Liam, Mac and Payne had broken away from all those years ago. We lived under-ground. We fought where we could. If I could only break these chains, I'd make a run for it. I'd find a way to get Finn, Jones and Rackham the hell out of here too.

"Is it cold down there?" Finn asked. His mind wandered like that, jumping from one thing to the next. He constantly asked me about the caves. I'd never confirmed nor denied their exis-tence to him. But, he knew. The wolves of Mammoth Forest had grown to legendary status all throughout Kentucky. It's the last thing we wanted.

"It's not so cold." It was as close as I would come to admitting anything to him. It was the only way I could protect the friends I'd left behind and the ones I had beside me.

"What will you do if the Alpha *does* come?" he asked.

"I don't want to think about that right now. Jesus, Finn. Are you going to just sit there and not mention what just happened?"

He moved again, rattling his chains. "What happened?"

Was he playing dumb? Had Buzzy hit him harder in the head the last time he questioned him than I realized?

I moved to the corner of my cell, bracing my back against the wall. "Finn, the girl. Who the hell was she?"

Finn went quiet for a beat. I leaned down so I could see him through the gap. Finn's hair hung in long, thin strings. It might have been dark at some point, but now he had thick patches of white running through it.

"You didn't see the woman outside just now?" I lowered my voice even further. Even mentioning her to Finn felt like a betrayal. But, my heart still thundered inside my chest. My flesh still burned where I'd touched her, no matter how briefly.

Finn's soft laughter infuriated me. "Yeah. I see her sometimes too. For me, she's tall and blonde with tits that don't quit. Sometimes she's wearing a metal bustier like she's some kind of Viking shield maiden. Yeah, I like that the best. Sometimes, she's a mermaid. Though, I always wondered how the hell that would work. Like is there a slit or something...or do you have to wait until she's got legs to..."

"Finn!" I banged my chains against the wall. "Stay with me, man. That's not what I'm talking about. She was real. I touched her. She was right outside. She talked to me."

"Oh, that's a good one then, brother. Hold on to that for a while."

Fuck. He still thought I was talking about some dream. Was I? Was she? I blinked hard, trying to clear my vision. Was the whole thing some pain-fueled vision? It felt so real. I could still smell her. I raised my hand to my face. I'd touched her with it.

She'd tried to pull away. On the back of my wrist, I had two faint lines where she'd dug her nails into me.

I moved, ready to slide that hand beneath the wall and show Finn so I could prove it to him. In the end, I decided against it. She was mine. Whether she was real or not, I would protect her.

"You're right," I said. "That was a good one."

Finn cleared his throat. "I didn't want to tell you this, man. After everything you've been through. But, if it were me I'd want to know. You need to get ready. Jones says the Alpha is coming. It's no joke. If Maestro can't get you to tell them anything about your resistance operation, the Alpha's ready to move to subjugate you. I'm sorry. I really am."

Squeezing my eyes shut, I slouched against the wall. Subjugation. If it were true, it meant I would betray everyone and everything I loved. It meant it was time to die.

FOUR

JETT

I tried to slip in while the rest of the girls slept. I should have known that plan would never work. Vera stood by the campfire, her eyes practically glowing with the same heat. She crossed her arms in front of her, standing stock still. As I adjusted the rifle on my back I moved toward the fire, stretching my hands out to warm them.

Vera struck like a snake. She got between me and the fire and shoved me back hard. "What the hell do you think you're doing?"

Melanie stirred. She lay curled on her side in her sleeping bag. She reached over and nudged Caroline. "What? What is it?" Caroline yawned and stretched. She at least had the decency to look miserable when her eyes focused in the dim light.

"Take your hands off me," I said to Vera, holding my hands up. I wasn't looking to throw down with her, but I would if she pushed me too hard.

"You went back there, didn't you?" she asked. Vera didn't even bother trying to keep her voice down. For as pissed as she was with me for going off on my own, she seemed ready to attract any stray members of the Pack patrol with her temper.

I slid the rifle strap off my shoulder and set it down. Pushing past Vera, I took a seat on a boulder close to the fire. Caroline sat up and unzipped her sleeping bag. Melanie helped her, scooping her up in her arms. Caroline's useless leg dangled over Melanie's forearm. She'd suffered a bad break a few weeks ago during our last close call with the Pack. We'd tried to set it, but it hadn't healed right. She grunted from the strain as she helped Caroline to her own spot by the campfire. When Melanie took a seat beside her, it was settled. We were doing this.

"Yes," I said, staring hard at Vera. She loomed over me, her toned arms gleaming white. She wore what she always did, a ripped black t-shirt and khakis, her hair shaved close to her head.

Vera kicked a branch into the fire. Sparks flew all around me. I stayed stone still. Let them burn. Vera didn't scare me. Well, that wasn't entirely true. Most days she scared the hell out of me. But, today wasn't most days.

"Vera, baby, take a knee," Melanie said to Vera. Caroline looked downright petrified. She'd been glorious the first day I met her. Tall, blonde, the stereotypical Midwest homecoming queen and cheerleading captain. We met during orientation, both us struggling to find our way around campus. That seemed a lifetime ago. Now, Caroline was pale and skinny. She too had cropped her once shining blond mane close to her head.

"I'd rather stand," Vera barked back. Her tone made Caroline jump. Melanie kept calm. It was her way. While the rest of us railed and argued, Melanie Dorchester quietly waited for the storm to pass. She'd then point out the most obvious, reasonable solution to whatever had stoked the flames in the first place. Today, I knew there'd be no such diplomatic counsel. What I'd done was a banishable offense. I did it anyway, and everyone here knew I'd do it again and why.

"Did you see anything?" Caroline asked the obvious question. That surprised me. She usually hated getting in the middle of Vera and me. She abhorred conflict of any kind.

I didn't answer right away. Instead, I kept my gaze locked with Vera's. She knew what I was thinking. Everyone here, including her, burned with the question Caroline had just asked.

"Sit down," I said. "Hear me out. Then if you want to kick my ass, you can try."

I knew she wouldn't sit. She might have if I hadn't told her to. Everything was a power play with Vera Way.

"Do you really need me to go over this again? Clearly you don't give the first shit about what happens to the rest of us. Sure, I can see why you'd probably be happy if the Pack came to rip my lungs out. What about Caro and Mel though? Huh? You realize they'd go down with me if those fuckers captured you or followed you back here?"

"Well," I said, "they didn't. Did they? They never even knew I was there."

That was only a half-truth. I'd been seen. I'd *let* myself be seen. The next time the Pack took Gunnar Cole in for questioning, he might tell them. Vera was right, but it didn't matter.

"Jett," Caroline spoke up. "Tell us what happened. Vera, it's over now. She's back. Everything's fine. Fight about it later."

Vera looked at Caroline like she'd just sprouted horns. Melanie put a hand over her mouth to hide her smile. Vera would go ballistic if she realized Melanie was taking sides against her right now. She wasn't, but Vera wouldn't see it that way. I didn't wait for Vera's permission. I never did.

"There's a new one, all right," I said. "I don't know how long he's been there. By the looks of him, it's probably been a few weeks."

"I knew it," Melanie said. "Vera, I *told* you! Did you see him? Is he one of them?" Melanie clutched Caroline's hand. Caroline grew very still. Tears made her eyes glisten. I knew what she felt. Part of her didn't want to hear my answer. It might let a glimmer of hope back into all of our hearts.

I swallowed hard, considering the best way to tell them this. A part of me wanted to keep it to myself for just a little bit longer. Gunnar's face swam in front of me. I'd seen so little of him. His eyes, his bruises. Glimpses of his strong, powerful body bent and broken. My breath caught and a tiny flame flickered inside of me. For the briefest of moments, when Gunnar took my wrist, the world seemed to stop. It was as if all the air left my body and when I inhaled again, my heartbeat wasn't my own. I *felt* his. Was that even possible?

My eyes drifted to Melanie. Of everyone here, she'd be the one to ask. I couldn't. If I even mentioned it, Vera would straight up lose her mind. I wouldn't put it past her to grab a stick from the fire and start swinging the glowing end at me. It wouldn't be me she'd be really trying to hurt. I was just the closest thing.

"I couldn't see much," I said, clearing my throat. "It was dark. I didn't want to risk shining a flashlight or anything."

Caroline reached for her sleeping bag. Unzipping it, she spread it over her legs. Even with the fire blazing in front of her, she had trouble regulating her body temperature. The circulation in her injured leg wasn't good. Melanie reached over to help her.

"There are four prisoners," I said. "The fifth cell is empty, I think. Six guards. Two on standing duty. The other four patrol. They're getting lazy about it though. There's a bunkhouse on the north end," I said. I picked up a stick and drew the layout of the prison camp as best I could remember. Only Vera had ever gotten close enough to see it in detail. And that was briefly and she'd been bleeding from a gunshot wound to her arm at the time.

"So the tunnels *do* go all the way to the camp," Caroline said. A smile brightened her face.

"They do," I said. "I surfaced about thirty feet away from the cells. There has to be more. Why would anyone have built the tunnels *to* the camp but not away?"

Vera and I had discovered the tunnel system under Carter Hollow near the Rockcastle River a year ago. It had been a game changer. Caroline theorized they'd been built by someone who'd escaped from the prison camp decades before. It mattered. If prisoners made them there was a chance the Chief Pack didn't know about them. We'd grown bolder over the last few months using them. But, the constant worry was that we were wrong and the Pack itself had built them. If so, it was only a matter of time before we ran into them.

"I plan to try finding out if there's another branch," I said. I purposely didn't look at Vera, but I could feel her eyes boring into my back nonetheless.

"You're back," she said, her tone softening. "You're safe. Look, no harm no foul. Let's just move on."

All three of us turned to stare at her. For Vera to have a change of heart that quickly was rare. When she got in a mood like this, she generally sulked for days.

"You know that's not going to happen," I said. This drew sharp gasps from both Caroline and Melanie.

Vera finally sat. She covered her face with her hands. Melanie reached over and rubbed her back. "Baby," she whispered. "Let Jett talk. You more than anybody should realize how much this means to her. If there's a chance that what we heard about Birch Haven is true, don't we have to find out?"

"I don't give a shit about Birch Haven anymore," Vera said, but her voice was choked. We all knew it was a lie. None of us could ever forget Birch Haven. We'd all gone there, thinking it would give us a fresh start at a better life than the ones we were born into. We'd been lured with scholarships that were too good to be true. At first, it had been perfect. Then, little by little, our friends started to disappear. Birch Haven College was nothing more than a breeding farm for members of the Chief Pack. Girls were taken against their will and marked by wolf shifters as mates. Three years ago, our group of twelve found a way out. We'd been on the run ever since, never able to get close enough to the border without the Pack finding us.

"I do care," Melanie answered for me. "I'm not saying it changes anything. I'm not saying we should be stupid about it." Melanie leveled a hard look at me. For the first time since I came back, I felt truly guilty. No matter what else I'd done, no matter how noble the cause, these women would have suffered if I hadn't come back or if the Pack found me.

"And you care too," Melanie went on.

"I made a promise," I said. They'd all heard this before, but Vera at least needed reminding. "Jade died in *my* arms, Vera. Her blood was on *my* hands. Maybe we were wrong. Maybe if we'd just let her go back to Birch Haven, she could have at least seen her sister one more time."

"I loved Jade as much as the rest of you did," Vera said quietly. "She was my roommate. She was the first person I met at orientation. But she's gone. We're not."

"Maybe," I said. "But if this prisoner is who we think he is, if he knows whether the rumors about Birch Haven are true, I need to be sure."

"It's a fool's errand," Vera said. "How many girls were still enrolled at that school last year, huh? Hundreds? What are the odds this fucker would even know who Jasmine Russell was?"

"That's not the point," Caroline said. "It's a lead, Vera. That's all. If this guy had a hand in liberating Birch Haven...if that really happened, don't you want to know? I know I do."

Vera straightened. She shrugged off Melanie's touch. "Not this way."

"Then how?" I said, throwing up my hands. "This *is* the way. And I'm sorry, but there are only two people capable of doing this, and I don't see you stepping up, Vera."

Everyone fell silent. I'd told the hard truth that Vera didn't want to. It was a low blow and I wasn't proud of it, but it had to be said.

"Jett," Melanie spoke up. "Be fair."

"I'm *being* fair. But what are we doing, huh? How long are we going to wander around in the dark? If Birch Haven is gone, we need to know how. We need to know what happened to those girls. We need to know what happened to Jade's sister. And, dammit, Vera, we need to know if there's a way to save Melanie."

Vera slowly rose. Her jaw trembled as she clenched it hard. Her fingers shook as she curled and uncurled her fists. Oh, she wanted to hit me. Hard.

"You think this prisoner has the answers to all that?"

"Maybe," I said.

"Did you see him? All of him? Did you see his chest?" Vera's voice grew quieter.

I let out a hard breath. I wished I had the answers she sought. The truth was, it had been too dark. I couldn't be sure whether Gunnar bore the mark of the resistance we'd heard of. Maybe Vera was right. This was a fool's errand. And yet, I couldn't shake the feeling that there was...something...something important about Gunnar Cole.

"I need to go back," I said. "I can do it. Vera, it was easy. In two hours of quiet waiting, I had the patrols down pat. They're lazy. It doesn't occur to them that there will *ever* be any trouble. The prisoners are weak. There haven't been any reports of uprisings in like a hundred mile radius. Let me see what I can find out."

"What if he sees you?" Caroline asked. "This prisoner. Just because the Pack wants to hurt him doesn't mean he's an ally. Who knows how they've twisted his mind or even why he's in their cage in the first place?"

"I know. I know all of that. And I know how thin my reasoning is going to sound. But, you know me. I'm not reckless. How many times have I proven that? How many times have I put my life before yours? How many times have I *saved* your lives?

Huh? Even yours, Vera. I don't want to die either. But, I made a promise to Jade that if I ever had the chance, I'd try and find her little sister. She *died* for us. We all owe her this. So, let me finish what I started. I'll be back in twenty-four hours. If I'm not, move the camp."

Vera dropped her head. Melanie reached up and curled her arm around the side of Vera's leg. There were tears in her eyes. It was as close to permission I'd ever get from her. Even though we both knew I didn't need it.

FIVE

JETT

I left at dusk the next night. I did it when Vera and the others went down to the lake to wash our clothes and bathe. It had been my job to watch the camp, but it was better to have me gone before they came back. I wouldn't put it past Vera to either try to talk me out of it or brain me with a cook pot when I wasn't looking just so she could tie me up and keep me here.

I stayed at the southern edge of the woods away from the known trails. The next town was two miles to the east. The Pack never patrolled this far out. This time, I left the larger rifle behind and settled for the smaller nine. I hoped to God I wouldn't have to use it. If I did, we'd lose our biggest asset against the Pack. But, I damn sure wasn't going to die over Gunnar Cole.

I took to the tunnels about two hundred yards from the prison camp. We'd mapped what we could, but these things could go for miles as far as we knew. I would love to know who built them. Vera and I had worked on expanding them even beyond

Carter Hollow. It was brutally hard work and we hadn't gotten far. But, it gave us both a way to direct our anger and Vera's hopelessness about Melanie's condition.

"He's got a day," a gruff voice said above my head. I froze as dirt rained down. Had I misjudged? The prison camp should be about fifty yards in front of me.

"You know what they call you, don't you?" A second man spoke. His voice had a lilt to it. I didn't quite recognize the accent.

The first man let out a bitter laugh. "And why should I give a shit what they call me?"

"You shouldn't. But, you might be proud of it, actually."

"Proud? You think too highly of them. They're not people, Mr. Lowell. They shouldn't even be called shifters. They're worse than scum."

"Maestro," Lowell said. "I don't know what it means. But it sounds, I don't know...respectful."

"Maestro means master, you idiot."

"No, I know that. I just don't understand the context."

Feet shuffled, more dirt rained down. I couldn't move. I couldn't dare breathe. What if they caught my scent? Fuck. After all this, it would kill me if Vera was right all along.

"Look," Lowell said. "This isn't over yet. You haven't failed."

The ground vibrated all around me. For a brief, terrifying moment, I thought the tunnel would cave in under the weight of the two shifters above me. They moved off though. I heard a sickening thud and a grunt of pain.

"I'm sorry," came Lowell's strangled cry.

"Who the fuck are you to judge success or failure where I'm concerned?"

The ground shook again. One of the men, Lowell I guess, retched. "You're taking it wrong. I'm an ass for saying it like that. I'm sorry. Why don't you just let the Alpha have him? Gunnar's a pile of shit. I've been here a long time. You're the best there is. Nobody's gonna deny that. But that fuck has been off the grid for a long time. He's not like the other pukes that come through here. So, let the Alpha have him. He's sending for Gunnar tomorrow. You'll be rid of him. Isn't that worth something?"

Maestro's voice moved further away. "It's worth nothing. You don't even know what you're talking about. If the Alpha subjugates him tomorrow, if he forces Pack control on him, he won't get the best of his mind. He'll weaken him. Trust me. We want him strong."

"Well, it's out of our hands. I say good riddance."

The two of them moved further away and I couldn't hear what they were saying. I'd heard enough. The Pack was coming for Gunnar Cole. One day more and he'd be one of them.

SIX

Gunnar

When I closed my eyes, I saw hers, wide and dark. My heart sparked with a tiny flame as I woke from the dream. For the first time since I'd come to Camp Hell, I felt no pain.

"You feel that?" Finn asked. His voice had a light quality I wasn't used to. He might be dreaming himself. He talked in his sleep all the time. Though, he usually didn't ask me questions. Mostly it was incomprehensible mumbling punctuated by brief bits of one-word insults.

"I'm right here, Finn," I answered. Reaching over, I tapped my hand under the wall.

"No, I'm serious. Listen." So he was awake after all. I went still, pricking my ears. The trees rustled outside as the wind changed direction. Further out, I scented a doe. She was a young one, anxious, scared. My stomach growled and my wolf woke. What I wouldn't give to hunt. Though, if I shifted now, I couldn't trust that I wouldn't bring the entire Pack down on my head. I'd been human so long, I might not be able to control it.

"I don't hear anything," I said. "You're losing it. Try to sleep."

"Sleep? The fuck you talking about? Someone's coming. Buzzy bash you in the head harder than usual this week? The patrols are out to the south. Somebody's coming from the north. Can't make it out. Shifters? Shit. This could be it, Gunnar!"

Finn let out a guttural cry that ripped through me. He was scared. Terrified. His chains rattled and I heard a commotion on the other side of him. Rackham had to sense Finn falling apart too. Sometimes he was better than me at calming Finn down.

I left them to it, settling back into the far corner of my cell. It was selfish of me. Finn needed help. I just didn't have the strength to provide it. Not tonight.

Whatever Rackham told him must have worked because the next sound to reach me was Finn's rhythmic snoring. Good. I hoped he had peaceful dreams tonight. I was just about to drift off myself when my heart flared with alarm.

You think you'll hold out. They all do. You won't. Don't think less of yourself for it.

The thoughts in my head weren't my own. My heart jackhammered as I tried to separate what was happening in my head from what was real.

They won't hold out, your friends. What are their names?

Finn. Rackham. Jones. The answers popped into my head unbidden. The voice had pulled them out somehow.

See? It doesn't hurt so much when you just give in. You don't have to hurt at all anymore.

I tried to keep my mind black. Panic began to seep up my spine. No. I couldn't let it. Instinct screamed back at me, telling me that's what he wanted. He. The Alpha. Oh, God. He was inside my head.

I slammed my skull against the wall, trying to drive him out. Where was he? I tilted my head trying to catch the wind. I couldn't scent anything unusual. His fading laughter rippled through me. Then, I was alone.

When I opened my eyes, it had gone pitch black. The clouds fully obscured the moon and only a few bright stars peeked out. Leaves crunched as uneven footsteps approached. It wasn't the Pack patrol or the guards. They moved with confident purpose. The owner of those footsteps was trying hard not to be heard.

I went flat on my belly and peered through the gap in the northern wall. She was good. I'll give her that. She knew how to time her steps with the rustling of the wind. She dressed dark, smearing her face with mud or paint to break up the line of her profile. To any animal out there, the whites of her eyes were the only thing she couldn't hide.

Please, God, I prayed. Please don't let me betray her. Let me be strong enough to fight the Alpha off. My head stayed silent. Whatever grip he'd had on me was gone. For now.

When her scent reached me full on, it drove the breath out of me, replacing it with scorching heat that raced up my spine and spread out to my fingertips. She stopped at the edge of the tree line, crouched low, then looked straight at me.

I didn't imagine it. It was the girl from the other night. Those brown eyes seared straight through me. She looked left and right, then came to me, staying low to the ground.

I couldn't help myself. I reached for her again, closing my fingers around her calf. I needed her. Though it made no sense, the closer she was, the easier it felt to stay out of my head. I was stronger when she was near.

She wore black pants tucked into heavy combat boots. The last time I'd touched her, she flinched. Tonight, she stayed stock still.

"Let go," she whispered. "Carefully, or the first shot goes straight between your eyes."

She leveled the barrel of a nine millimeter straight at me, keeping it just out of my reach. Smart. Even in my current state, if she were any closer, there was no way she could squeeze that trigger faster than I could disarm her.

"You think that'll kill me?" I asked, struggling to keep my voice low enough so the others wouldn't hear. It seemed to matter to her too. She'd come to the eastern corner of my cell, away from everyone else. Still, I worried that they'd hear or sense her. That should have mattered to me because I wanted to keep them safe. But, the opposite was true. I didn't want anyone else near her.

"Who are you?" I asked. I carefully lifted my fingers off her leg. I half expected her to run. She didn't. Instead, she squatted in front of the wall, keeping her hand steady on the nine, the other dangling over her knee.

"I'm going to ask the questions for now," she answered.

I let out a low laugh. I'd heard that line so many times from so many different torturers since I came here. Common sense said she must just be another one. Brute force hadn't worked to get me to betray the Mammoth Forest wolves. Of course they'd try a lighter touch in a more appealing package.

"Gunnar Cole," she started. "You said that was your name. For now, I think I'll believe you."

"Thanks," I whispered. Finn stirred on the far side of his cell and my heart dropped. No. It was better if this girl got gone before even Finn knew she was here. I tilted my head, straining to look up at her from my vantage point on the ground. What I wouldn't give to be able to smash through this fucking wall and get to her.

"There isn't a lot of time," she said, cognizant of Finn's movements. "So, I'll be quick. There's one thing I want to know."

"And exactly why would I want to tell you anything? What's in it for me? You gonna shoot me with that thing? I'll admit, it'll sting a bit. You might even get lucky and I'll hold still long enough for you to shoot me between the eyes. It'd have to be a one in a million shot though to actually kill me. I don't know if you've heard, but my kind isn't so easy to kill."

She dropped from her knees to her belly, putting her face in the wall gap. It got hard for me to breathe. Those dark eyes of her swirled with fury. She was stunning. I'd sensed that, but now I could actually see it. She had a hard beauty with a sharp nose, high cheekbones and lips so full I wanted to taste them.

"And you don't know a thing about my kind, Gunnar Cole."

I stayed very still, afraid that if I moved, even to blink, I would spook her and she'd run. As much as I feared for her safety, I *needed* her here, just for a few minutes more at least.

"Fair enough," I said. "So what's your question? I'm curious."

"Birch Haven," she answered. It took me off guard. Of course I expected her to ask me about my companions in Mammoth Forest. It's all the Maestro or any of the Pack torturers cared about. Where did I come from? How many of us were there? Where did we hide? Who was helping us from the outside?

"Sounds lovely," I said, resting my chin on my hands. I had to be careful. The longer I looked into her eyes, the less I'd be able to hide the turmoil swirling behind mine. I couldn't let her know she affected me. I had to stay indifferent. Slowly, achingly, I made myself sit up. More than anything, I just wanted to slip my hand through that gap in the damn wall and touch her. For now, I had to settle for the comfort of hearing her breathing.

"Is it still there? I've heard rumors and I need to know if they're true."

The question stunned me. If she were working for the Pack, she should know by now how we'd liberated Birch Haven. Had the Pack managed to keep it secret? That seemed impossible. It could all be another trick, of course. Get me to believe she wasn't in the know, I'd be more likely to think she wasn't sent here by the Pack itself. It couldn't be a coincidence that I'd just heard the Alpha in my head, then she showed up. And yet, there was something so desperate and hungry about her tone. Every instinct in me told me she wasn't a friend of the Pack.

"What's your name?" I asked.

"I'm not..."

"Right," I cut her off. "You're the one asking the questions. Only, you want something from me. Seems to me I don't need a damn thing from you."

It killed me to say that to her. My body screamed the truth. Oh, I needed something from her. I needed her touch. I needed to see her face. My heart thundered with that need and my legs felt weak. Who the hell was this girl? She wasn't a shifter, and yet there was something unusual about her. She was purely human, and yet, I'd never been around another human who had affected me like this. It had to be me. It had to be the Alpha's hold. I'd been in pain so long, cut off from the people I cared about for so long...I was looking for something that just straight up wasn't there.

This had all the hallmarks of something Maestro would do. She was his pawn, his latest ploy to get into my head. It had to be.

"Jett," she said in a breathless rush. "People call me Jett."

I squeezed my eyes shut, imagining her face swimming before me. Jett. Jett. Jett.

"Who sent you here, Jett?"

"No," she answered sharply. "Now you. Birch Haven. I want to know what happened there."

"Well, see, that's a pretty big ask. And it would seem to me there are probably other people in better positions than me to tell you about something like that. Why me? Huh? Why not just take a drive out there and see for yourself?"

"Listen, Gunnar Cole," she said, her voice rising.

"Keep your voice down, Jett," I said, loving the sound of her name on my lips. "I don't know who sent you, but I'm guessing you're not too keen on attracting the Pack patrols. At least, that's what you want me to believe."

"You have a hell of a lot more to fear from the Pack patrols than I do," she said. "And you're just about out of time. You know what's going to happen, don't you? You know what they're planning to do with you?"

My throat ran dry. I'd heard this before from Finn. I was next on the list for subjugation. Her telling me now just lent credence to the theory she was one of Maestro's or the Alpha's manipulations. Her gun gleamed in the moonlight and my heart thundered so loud I felt sure she could hear it.

I went back to my belly and reached for Jett. She didn't try to move this time when I reached for her wrist. Electricity seemed to spark between us when my fingers made contact with her skin. Her breath hitched and I could see tiny beads of sweat on her upper lip.

Holy shit. It wasn't just me. I wasn't imagining it. There was something about this girl. My pulse spiked. I ran my thumb along the underside of her wrist, feeling the tiny webbing of veins there. It took a second, maybe two, but this wasn't some trick. Her pulse fluttered where I touched her, rising to match mine.

Jett jerked her hand away. "Stop that! I don't know what you're doing, but don't. Can you help me or not?"

"Help you?" It was such an odd way to phrase it. How was answering her question about Birch Haven helping her? Did she not understand what that place was or even what kind of danger she was in now?

"Forget about Birch Haven," I said. "That's the last place a girl like you needs to go anywhere near."

She crouched lower so I could see her eyes. They flamed with indignation, setting off a new round of jackhammering inside my chest. "It's too late for that."

Her words were a blow. My blood ran cold. Birch Haven had been a prison for girls like her. Hell, it was probably worse for them than Camp Hell was for me. The students of Birch Haven

College had been used as nothing more than breeding stock for the Alpha's whims. But, we'd changed all that, hadn't we? The one hope I clung to, the thing that got me through most days was the knowledge that Mac and Payne had gotten those women out of there and burned the place to the ground. So, why was Jett so interested in knowing about it?

"Tell me why you want to know about Birch Haven. What's that place to you?"

Hard laughter reached my ears from the east. The guards were headed back this way. "You have to get out of here," I said, my voice tearing from me.

"You have to answer what I asked you." Her eyes widened with desperation. She made a nervous glance to the east toward the voices. Squinting, she raised her weapon toward the sound.

"No! You start shooting now, you'll draw them all down here."

"Who the hell are you talking to?" Finn whispered. "Gunnar, what's going on?"

Jett froze, her eyes locked with mine. She was truly scared. If she was Maestro's, she was *very* good.

"Go back to sleep," I said. "I had that dream again. The one about the woman with the dark eyes."

"Mmmm," Finn said. "Sounded like a good one. The girl with the great tits and the black hair? How far'd you get this time?" Finn's laughter was a good sign. At the same time, my heart dropped as Jett's pale skin colored.

"Yeah," I answered, enjoying the effect it had on her. "That girl. And the rest of it's none of your business. Go back to sleep. I'll tell you all about it in the morning."

Finn went quiet for a second. Then, his tone went dark. "I hope so, man. I really hope so. Jones says the top brass is coming the day after. Heard it straight from Legs. You suppose they're fucking with us? I don't know, man. Maybe I'm finally losing it, but I can *feel* 'em getting closer. Can't you?"

Jett dropped my gaze. She tilted her head toward Finn, straining to hear what he said. It meant something to her because she let out a sigh and her lids grew heavy.

"Who knows?" I answered. "But they're *always* fucking with us. No sense in worrying about rumors. The shit in front of us on a daily basis is bad enough."

"I don't know how you do it. How the hell you can keep your head on straight when you know they're coming for you...you give me hope, man."

"Sorry about that," I said, staring straight at Jett.

Finn let out a few more rumbles, but his chains quieted and I knew he'd turned back to the wall. In another second, he'd start snoring. The Pack patrols moved off as well, likely heading south before they doubled back and hit the western perimeter. If Jett left now and headed north, she could be far away before they got here. That is, if she were truly trying to avoid getting caught. On the other hand, maybe they knew all along she was here.

"It's not a rumor," she finally said, leaning close to the gap in the wall. I inhaled as she exhaled, drinking in her scent. I had to be careful. The urge to touch her face, to run my thumb along her bottom lip burned strong. If I gave into it, I risked getting her scent on me. If the guards caught it, they could track her.

"I know you know what happens when the Alpha comes for

you," she said. "That's why you're in this cell, isn't it? You figured out a way to live on the outside for a while. Listen, I don't care about that. I don't care if your people and the Pack rip each other apart. I just need to know what happened at Birch Haven. That's all."

"Why?"

Jett hesitated. Her eyes flickered as she worked out whether to tell me more. "I had friends there." I knew it cost her something to reveal that much. My heart broke a little wondering who those friends might be. I wanted to take away the pain in her eyes. But, something else burned inside of me even stronger.

"Do you know how to get that one in a million shot?" I asked.

Jett's lips parted. She seemed a little shocked by the question. I flicked my eyes to her gun. The idea came suddenly, making dangerous hope flare. He'd touched my mind. Maybe I wouldn't be strong enough to push him out next time.

"Tell me, Jett. You think you know how to kill a wolf?"

She looked down then let her fingers trail over the barrel of her gun. "I know exactly how to kill a wolf."

"And you think you really know what happens to me if the Alpha shows up?"

She snapped her hard gaze back to me. "Yes. Just like I know what happens to the women in places like Birch Haven."

"Good," I said, my pulse rising again. I saw the tiny pulse in her temple flicker to match it.

Voices rose in laughter again. Shit. The patrol had changed course. We had no more time. They were headed this way. Jett heard it too and drew her legs up until she squatted near the gap in the wall, ready to pop up and run.

"Tell me!" she said, raising her voice as much as she dared.

"I'll do that for you," I said, cold resolve hardening around my heart like cement. I hadn't planned this. I had no plan at all until Jett presented me with one. I would not allow myself to be subjugated to the Pack. I would not let the Alpha any further into my mind. No matter what.

"Hurry," she said.

"You hear something?" One of the guards said as he stopped. Leaves crunched beneath his feet. Jett's eyes widened in terror.

"Hurry," she mouthed.

I raised a finger to my lips. "Come back tomorrow night. I'll tell you everything you want to know on one condition."

"Name it." I reached for her, grabbing her wrist. She tried to pull away.

"I'll give you every detail about what happened at Birch Haven. Because I *was* there. Wherever you heard that rumor, consider it a reliable source."

"Is it there? Did they get out? Tell me what you saw!"

I smiled. "Tomorrow night. I'll tell you. But you have to promise me to take that one in a million shot afterward."

"What?" Her skin went pale again.

"I'll tell you about Birch Haven if you promise to kill me."

Jett's throat constricted as she took a hard swallow. As the voices grew nearer, she gave me a slow nod. "All right," she said. "You have a deal. One in a million, Gunnar."

"That's right. Now run."

She did. Her hair flew behind her as her boots crunched on the ground. They were coming. God. They would see her. Then, just like the night before, Jett disappeared straight through the ground.

SEVEN

JETT

"You are *not* thinking straight!"

I expected this from Vera. Hell, I even expected it from Melanie. But, when Caroline began to shout, I knew I'd lost them all.

"What was I supposed to do, shoot him right there?"

"No," Vera said. She stood apart from us. We'd gone down to the lake. Vera had her hand on an elm tree, picking at the bark. "You're not supposed to shoot him. You weren't supposed to be seen at all. That was the deal, wasn't it? You were just gonna do recon, see if there were any new prisoners, how far the tunnel went. If you were lucky, maybe you'd hear bits and pieces that might be helpful. Now, you've made contact with this guy. He knows who you are, your scent."

"He's not going to..." I stopped myself. What had I been about to say? That he wasn't going to hurt me? That I knew him, knew his heart? Yes. That's exactly what I had been about to say. I also knew how crazy it would sound to the rest of them.

Shifters were the enemy. They'd been luring women to them for years, taking them against their will. We'd all seen it. We'd all lost friends and family, people we loved. Shifters did that. They were to blame.

"You don't know what he's going to do," Melanie said. She was calmer than Caro or Vera. She kept her cool eyes on me, sitting on a rotted log next to Caroline. Melanie had a hand on Caro's back.

"He could have shouted," I said. "He could have called the guards, or even drawn the attention of the prisoner in the cell next to him. He didn't do that. He even covered for me when his cellmate thought he heard something."

"That means nothing," Melanie said. "Jett, come on. I've seen this before. We all have. They don't ever come at you hard at first. Well, most of them don't. It's more subtle."

She rose from the log and walked toward me. I kept my position against another oak tree, pressing my back into it hard. I looked away, wishing I could transport myself anywhere but here. If only it were that easy. We'd all heard stories that things were better outside of Kentucky. The Pack's reach extended only so far. But, every time we'd ever tried to cross the border, we lost someone. Jade had been the last. My tears started to flow, bursting out of me unbidden. This was for her. All of it was for her.

"Jett," Melanie said, softer. She stood right in front of me. Vera kept a watchful stare, ever protective of Melanie, even from me. She put a light hand on my arm. "Jett, look at me."

Gritting my teeth, I did. Melanie had such a kind face with big, sad, blue eyes. She wore her blonde hair long, even in the sticky heat of summer. Smiling, she gathered her hair in one hand and turned so I could see the back of her neck. Melanie had a jagged, cruel scar at the nape. The edges were puckered and purple. It was a bite mark. Three years ago, a shifter had done that to her, binding him to her for life. It was a miracle that she managed to run away. Every day, she lived with the fear that he would find her. We all did. Keeping Melanie with us was a risk we took every single day.

"He was nice to me at first too," Melanie said, letting her hair drop. "I thought he was my friend. He wasn't like the rest of the men in Birch Haven. Quiet, reserved. He even took a beating for me. Did I ever tell you that? A group of shifters came after me, taunting me. Powell got in their faces. They outnumbered him four to one. They beat him so badly I thought he was dead. I thanked him. I thought I owed him something. He said he was going to get me out. Because, by then, I knew what that place was. He made me trust him. Then, he did this. It made him worse than the others, Jett. Because Powell made me believe there was hope and that there were others out there that weren't like the Birch Haven shifters. It's a lie though. This Gunnar? He's lying to you too."

I had a dozen arguments inside of me. I knew what the shifters of Birch Haven were like. I'd made friendships too only to see them twist into something else. I'd been lied to. Betrayed. I'd seen everything Melanie had except I'd been lucky enough to never be bitten. Of those of us who were left, Melanie alone bore that particular burden.

"I can handle it." I heard the words come out of my mouth and knew exactly what it sounded like to the rest of them. I'd let myself feel hope again.

Vera threw her hands up. Before this little intervention started, Caroline and Melanie had made her promise to stay silent. The good cops were going to have a crack at me first. I had to give her credit for staying out of it for this long.

"Look," I said, pushing myself off the tree. "I get it. Believe me. He's a shifter. That makes him no different than any of the rest of them we've known. Except for one thing. He's in *that place*. I'm not going to go so far to say the enemy of my enemy is my friend. Guys, I'm not stupid or naive. The fact that I'm still standing here breathing tells you that. But, he's not part of the Pack. I know that for sure. He thinks for himself. For now. As long as that's true, he's of use to us."

"I'll make this simple," Vera said. "You're not going back there. Not ever. None of us are. It was a decent plan at first. If there had been a way to learn something about Birch Haven, we needed to try. You did. And you gave us more information about the tunnels than we had before. It was a success, Jett. I'm grateful. You're a badass for all of that. But, it's done now. We're moving on."

"We?" I asked. When Caroline and Melanie dropped their eyes, my back went up. There was something they weren't telling me.

Vera put a hand up when Melanie tried to go to her. Of course, they'd preplanned this before too.

"We've been in Carter Hollow too long," Vera said. "It's time to head north, or maybe south. We've gotten complacent. It's only a matter of time before the Pack figures out we're here. If Birch Haven *is* gone, that might make things even more complicated.

At least when they had that place…they were less likely to look for people like us."

Everything Vera said made sense. It was something we'd talked about for weeks. We'd survived on our own this long in part because we stayed moving. Still, the thought of leaving Carter Hollow left a cold space in my heart. I walked along the beach. I don't even think I made a conscious choice to do it, but I kept on walking.

I went up the hill, down an embankment, then stopped when I got to the small clearing on the north side. Deep in the Daniel Boone Forest, apple trees grew wild here in a place they shouldn't. Some bird or other animal had probably brought the seeds here decades ago. They'd already borne their fruit for the year and several rotted, brown apples littered the ground. This seemed odd to me. Why hadn't a squirrel or some other critter made off with them? It was almost as if the trees themselves had left them as an offering and the animals understood why.

I stood in front of the tallest tree and slowly squatted down. I brushed the fallen leaves out of the way and pressed my palm flat to the cool ground. Vera came up behind me. I wished she'd stay away for just a few minutes. She didn't even seem able to give me that much peace.

"I know," Vera said, her voice taking on an uncharacteristically soft tone. She put her hand on my shoulder.

"She was the best one of us," I said, sniffing back the tears that wanted to fall all over again.

"I know that too."

I looked up at Vera. "She died for me. Do you know that? That wolf was coming for me. Jade threw herself in his way. If she hadn't, I'd be dead and you could have buried me here instead of her. And you know what? It wouldn't have changed anything. You'd still be right here. Jade would be the one making runs to that prison camp and chasing down leads about her sister. I promised her, Vera. I *promised* her. It was the only thing that gave her any comfort that night. She died slow. You didn't know that. Slow and painful. She stayed sharp the entire time. I think that was the worst thing."

"Don't," Vera said. "Don't tell me any more. I know enough."

"That's just it. You don't know anything. Neither do I. Jasmine was in that fucking place. I know it, you know it, Jade knew it. I will keep my promise to her. No matter what."

"No matter what? Are you kidding me? Jett, give me a break. If Jade were here right now, you know what she'd say? She'd tell you that you don't risk the living for the dead."

"Jasmine's not dead! At least, we don't know that."

Vera shrugged. "She's either dead, marked, or she got away. What difference does it make? If she's dead or marked, we can't help her. If she got free, then we need more help than she does."

"I need to know!" I yelled, rising. "For Jade, I need to know. Dammit, I will know. You of all people. How the hell can you say we can't help her if she's been marked? You ready to say that about Melanie? Come on, Vera."

"My life, Melanie and Caro's lives, it's not worth the cost of that knowledge. Yours isn't either. Shit, Jett. It's you and me. You know that. Caroline's leg is getting worse. A wolf did that to her."

"She fell out of a fucking tree, Vera!"

"Running from a filthy shifter. And Melanie, every night I lie awake terrified that the one who marked her is going to come back for her. She still *feels* him. She's never told you that, but she tells me. I hold her in my arms when she cries out at night. Her scar burns with fever. She says that's him. He's trying to pull her back, and God, Jett. She wants to go! I'm terrified that one of these nights she will. We cannot stay here. The longer we do, the easier it will be for the Pack to find us. You know that. And I can't keep Caro and Mel safe by myself. I need you. You're the only one as strong as I am. Hell, you're stronger. You think I don't know that? We have to take care of them. We can't take care of Jade anymore. She's gone."

I stepped back, shaking my head. "I'm sorry. I'm so sorry. But, I have to do this. I have to know about Birch Haven. If it's been burned to the ground like we think, then there's hope. I could use a little hope, couldn't you?"

"No," Vera said coldly. "Hope is the last thing I need."

I crossed my arms in front of me. "Then I'm sorry for you. I really am. You're right about something. I am stronger than you are. I also know I can do this. I'm not leaving you, Vera. I'm coming back."

"But you're going," she said, defeated. "You're going back to that camp."

I sucked in a deep breath then slowly let it out. "I am."

Vera dropped her shoulders in defeat. "Then you need to know, we may not be here when you get back. I won't risk it."

"You think I'm under his spell?" I asked. "You think I'd do anything to put you at risk?"

"You already have."

Vera threw up her hands and started walking away. Her eyes glistened with unshed tears. In all the years since we'd been on the run together, I think it was the first time I'd ever seen her moved that way. It pulled at my heart and scared me.

When Vera disappeared through the trees, I turned back to Jade's grave. Everything Vera said made sense. I probably would have said those same things if the roles had been reversed. But, this was *my* role, not hers. When I had nothing left, I knew I could at least keep my promises.

Another promise made me rise.

My heart thundered inside of me. A slow, steady pulse ran through me. It felt different, but a part of me somehow. My head swam with it. When I closed my eyes, I could feel Gunnar's touch on my wrist, a slow, irresistible burn.

When I opened my eyes again, I could see the moon. It was time to go. I had one more promise to keep.

EIGHT

GUNNAR

They left me alone for most of the day. That was a bad sign. Then, they took me out of my cell. That was an even worse sign.

"Come on!" It wasn't Maestro or Legs or even Buzzy asking. Two guards, Lowell and Henny, showed up clanging a lead pipe against the rusted bars in the square cut out of my door. The sound grated, ringing through my bones. Finn groaned on his side of the cell. His fingers splayed out beneath the wall. He was having a really bad day. He hadn't kept what passed for a meal down in over twenty-four hours. I was starting to get worried.

"Get on your feet," Lowell said. He was the biggest guy in the camp other than me. Or at least, what I used to be. I hadn't seen a mirror in months, but my hipbones jutted out and my skin hung slack everywhere else. I was muscle and bone, nothing more.

Lowell had a voice that didn't match his stature. It was high-pitched with a lateral lisp. He was burly, like a lumberjack, with dark hair and yellow eyes that burned gold when he couldn't keep his wolf under control. Not one of these men had ever shifted around me. There had to be a reason for that. My guess was that the powers that be feared it would stir the prisoners too much. We'd be harder to control. There was always the possibility that the shift itself might kill one of us. From what little I could see of Finn beneath the wall, I didn't see how he'd physically survive it.

I thought about giving Lowell a hard time. I ached so badly from yesterday's session with Maestro, I just didn't have it in me. He'd flown into a rage when my blindfold slipped. I didn't see his face, but it didn't matter. My ribs were taking longer to heal today. Even a kick from Lowell might send me over the edge. I hauled myself up to my feet, dragging the dragonsteel chains behind me.

"Miss me already?" I asked, my voice scratchy and dry. They hadn't brought any of us dinner today. That right there should have been another bad sign if I'd had the energy to recognize it at the moment.

"Shut the fuck up, Gunnar," Henny said. He opened the door. Henny was tall, skinny with long, stringy hair. He almost looked like he could have been a prisoner once himself for as dirty as he was. For all I knew, maybe he was. He stank too. Even Lowell wrinkled his nose when Henny got too close.

It was in me to ask what was going on, but something made me stop. I didn't want to know. I didn't want to give either of these assholes the chance to goad me anymore. For as hungry as I was, I felt mentally stronger today than I had in months. Jett was the reason. She'd kindled something deep inside of me, even though I knew that was dangerous.

She might be dangerous. There was still every possibility that she was another one of Maestro's head games despite my gut feeling.

"It's your lucky day," Lowell said. "You're moving up in the world, Gunnar."

"Gunnar?" Finn's voice filled with panic. That was unusual for him. I wanted to chalk it up to whatever sickness seemed to grip him.

"Take it easy, Finn," I said, trying to make a joke of it. I caught a glimpse of Finn through the square in his door while Lowell led me out. What I saw made my heart lurch. Finn was losing weight, fast. He had angry sores on his wrists, ankles and elbows from where he rested on the floor and his chains scraped. His color was all wrong, sallow and gray. But, when Finn locked eyes with me, I almost dropped. One was brown and red-rimmed. The other glinted gold. I'd never seen that before. One human eye, the other all wolf. It didn't usually happen like that. There was something very, very wrong with Finn. This wasn't sickness; I feared it was brain damage.

"Where are you taking him?" Finn yelled.

"Not your business," Henny answered. "Go back to sleep while you can. You look like kooky-eyed shit."

"It's okay, Finn," I said raising a hand, I put a finger to my lips. "Don't worry about anything."

"You don't get it," Finn said. He found the strength to rise. He curled his fingers around the rusted bars and pressed his fore-head to them. "This is what they do, man. Are you taking him to the pit?"

Lowell looked back. He answered with a smile. Well, shit. I

didn't know what the pit was, but was pretty sure I didn't want to go there. Ever.

"Don't let 'em take you there. Gunnar! They don't come back from the pit." Finn started to scream it. "You go in as you, you come out as Pack!"

My heart turned to stone. I'd been hearing the rumors all week. The Alpha was coming. This was it.

Henny banged his stick on Finn's door. Finn jumped back and stumbled. He didn't have the strength to stand anymore. Henny and Lowell led me past Finn's cell. For the first time in all the months since they brought me here, I saw into the other cells as well.

Rackham was next. He sat in the corner of his cell, knees drawn up. When our eyes met, his were cold and dark. He had a mass of reddish hair and a long, unkempt beard. He raised his chin and gave me a slow, solemn nod. Next to him was Jones. So he was real after all. Jones stood tall and defiant in the center of his cell. His eyes flashed silver as the guards pushed me forward. Jones had blond hair slicked back with sweat. His body was covered with angry welts in a familiar pattern. They were from Maestro. Jones raised his fist, knuckles out, as I went by. I raised mine back.

"Enough," Lowell said, pushing me forward. The fifth cell was empty. They led me away, to the other side of the camp. A single cell stood all alone. It looked no different than the others: four cement footers beneath walls that didn't quite reach the ground. The rusted metal door had a small opening near the middle covered by bars. It was slightly bigger than the others, maybe ten by ten.

Henny opened the cell door while Lowell shoved me inside. He looped my chains through a giant metal ring bolted to the floor, all of it made of dragonsteel. I tested the strength, but it was no use.

"Relax," Lowell said. "I promise this time tomorrow things will start looking up for you. You might even say it's your lucky day."

I couldn't muster a response and didn't want to give Lowell the satisfaction of knowing I was worried. But, as the door clanged shut, my mouth felt as though I'd swallowed ash. Lowell could only mean one thing by his taunting. If he was telling the truth, he figured I'd be subjugated into the Pack sometime in the next twenty-four hours.

The thing that scared me most was that a part of me *wanted* it. It *would* be so much easier. I'd felt and fought against the pull of the pack so many times. It called to me like a siren song. There would be no more pain, no reason to fight, I could give over to it, finally. I could have peace.

The price of that peace chilled me to my core. Subjugated wolves lived and breathed for the Alpha. He could make me fight for him, kill for him. And he could make me betray the people I cared about no matter how much my soul fought against it.

Now you're thinking clearly. They're not friends, Gunnar. You don't need friends.

My heart dropped. No. No. No. I wouldn't do it. The urge to conjure my friend's names and faces pulled at me. He wanted their location most of all. I wouldn't do it. I would not do it.

You know me. If you just let yourself believe it. I'm not your enemy. What I do I do for the strength of all of us.

"What you do you do for you? You're sick. You kill innocent wolves and hurt women. For what?"

You can't see the big picture. I can. Everything I've done makes us stronger. We've been hunted and cursed for so many years. I can undo all of that. I can bring back the she-wolves.

"No one can. Anything you try isn't natural. It's twisted. It's evil."

Again, the Alpha's soft laughter drove out all other sounds. In the back of my mind, I knew the more I engaged with him, the stronger his hold might become. I quieted my thoughts. He held strong for a few moments, then quietly faded away.

Gathering my chains, I backed into a corner off the cell. Could I get them around my neck? I scanned the top of the cage in the dark. Was there a hook, a ledge? Anything I could brace it on? The walls were smooth. The metal loop in the wall kept the chains taut. I had enough slack to move against the wall, but not enough to wrap it around my neck.

One horrible night, I'd heard Finn try to bash his own head against the wall. It was early in my stay here. I'd tried to reason with him. Now, I understood the desperation he felt better than anyone. I tried it again, hitting the wall harder than the night before. I'm not proud. But shifters have heads harder than concrete. It made my ears ring, but little more. Besides, even if I'd cracked my own skull, it wouldn't be enough to kill me, and I healed too quickly.

"Shit," I whispered as I felt sticky, warm blood pour down the back of my neck.

"Knock it off. You're no good to me unconscious!" Jett's whisper hit me like a thunderbolt. Her eyes glinted in the gap in the wall where she crouched low to peer in at me.

With my ringing ears, I'd never even heard her approach. Was this the Alpha sending her to me again? Twice in a row, she'd appeared after I drove him out of my head. My pulse rocketed and I scrambled closer to the wall to get to her.

"What the hell are you doing here? The guards just left. They're going to find you!"

Jett's white teeth gleamed in the darkness as she smiled. "I'm smarter than I look. You let me worry about the guards. You made a deal with me. I came to collect."

Letting out a sigh, I pressed my head against the wall. Jett crouched beneath the opposite wall, too far for me to reach her. As the throbbing in my head began to subside, I craved her touch, knowing instinctively that it would soothe me.

"Come here," I said. "I can't hear you very well."

"That's your own fault."

"Yeah, it is. I still want you to come closer. I will not risk the guards hearing either one of us."

Jett disappeared. A few seconds later, her hand slid beneath the wall close to me. Still out of my reach, but close enough I could hear her heart beating. It had been a lie. She could have stayed a hundred yards away and my wolf ears would have picked up every whispered word. I had the sense she knew that but chose to get close to me anyway.

"So, tell me what I need to know," she said. "You made me a promise. I want to know about Birch Haven. What happened there?"

Snorting, I shifted my weight and slid lower so she could see my face. "You know what that place was? What they did to girls like you there?"

"That's not what I asked you. Is it still standing?"

I don't know why I hesitated. She was right; I had made her a promise. But, when I told her everything I knew, she might not have a reason to stay. Of course, that was better for her. Safer. And yet, my need to stay close to her burned through me.

"I don't know," I finally answered. "That's the truth. But yes, I was there. There was a battle. That's when I got captured."

Jett let out a choked sob. "The women. Tell me what happened to the women. Did you see?"

I squeezed my eyes shut trying to conjure up my last few minutes of freedom before the Alpha's guards captured me. "It was chaos. But yes, they got away. I don't know how many. Dozens. Fifty, sixty, maybe more. They broke through the gates and ran into the woods. Some got out on foot. Others were in vans."

"You saw that?" Jett was openly sobbing now and my heart broke. More than anything, I wanted to pull her into my arms. I wanted to inhale the sweet scent of her hair as she leaned against my chest.

"Yes," I said. "I saw that." There was more. I could tell her how Mac and Payne and I waited by the riverbank. Mac had someone working with him on the inside. His sister Lena had been there. I was pretty sure she was one of the ones who'd gotten out along with Mac's mate, Eve. There were others, but I couldn't see their faces in my mind as clearly. The Alpha's body-guard had hit me hard, cracking my jaw. I rounded on him and killed him. Payne had gotten hurt badly. At first I feared he was dead. But, as the Alpha's other guards overtook me, Payne locked eyes with me. He was alive. Thank God, he was alive.

"I saw a fire," I said. "I don't know who set it. It could have been my people, or one of the girls. Hell, it might even have been the Pack. They swarmed the place. I told you. It was chaos." I was careful not to say or think anything the Alpha didn't already know.

"But, they got out," Jett said, her voice taking on a dreamlike quality. What I wouldn't give to see her face full on. For now, it was enough that I could feel her rapid pulse beating in time with mine. I don't think she was aware of it. She hung on my words. For a moment, she had a trancelike quality as if she were trying to picture what I'd told her.

"You were from there," I said. Horror filled my heart. It would make sense of why Jett cared so much about what happened to Birch Haven. She knew what it was because she'd seen it first-hand. Rage rose within me, squeezing my heart. Had she been marked by one of the Alpha's men? Had she been touched against her will or hurt? My vision darkened. Jett's eyes flicked to mine and I knew she could see my wolf shining within. I'm told they are silver, though I've never seen them myself.

Jett's hand disappeared. I heard something crinkle, like stiff paper. She slid a tattered rectangle under the wall. "Tell me if you recognize her."

I took the paper from her, letting my fingers brush hers. Again, that electric spark shot from her heart to mine. She pulled away as if touching me burned her. Slowly, I picked up the photo-graph and squinted into the darkness. It was one of those cheesy class photographs on a blue background with an American flag in the corner. A pretty, light-skinned African-American girl smiled back at me. A mass of beautiful braids framed her face and inquisitive dark eyes. In this picture, she couldn't be much more than fifteen or sixteen.

"Who is she?" I asked.

Jett hesitated, then finally answered. "Her name was Jasmine."

"She was at Birch Haven?" I asked.

"Yes. I need to know if she was one of the ones who got out."

I slid the photograph back to her. "I'm sorry. I don't know. *I* didn't get out. The Pack caught me during the battle. I don't know what happened after I got separated from my..."

I stopped myself from saying the rest of it. I couldn't reveal the final truth to this girl. There was still the very real possibility she was working for the Pack. Though my heart and instinct told me no, I couldn't risk betraying Mac and the others.

I dropped my head and closed my eyes. In twenty-four hours, it wouldn't matter anymore. If I was still alive when the Alpha got here for real, my mind would no longer be my own.

When I opened my eyes, Jett's hand lay flat on the ground, still covering this Jasmine's photograph. I reached for her with snake-like speed, circling my fingers around her wrists. Jett clenched her fists and tried to pull away.

"I've held up my end," I said, my voice dropping an octave. "Time to hold up yours."

Jett froze. "One in a million shot."

"I'll hold still," I said with a bitter laugh. Jett put her other hand under the wall. In it, she held her nine millimeter. I'd have to lie flat on my belly, sliding as close to the gap as I could. She had a silencer twisted on the end, but the shot would still make plenty of noise. The same shot that would free me from subjugation might put her at even greater risk. Every protective instinct in me flared hot. Could I do that to her? Would my freedom be worth her safety?

Voices rose on the other side of the camp. Finn's scream was so loud it reached me just as if he were still in the cell next to me. My head grew foggy and started to buzz. Beneath all of that though, that familiar pull started dead center in my chest. My limbs went slack and it got hard to breathe.

"They're coming," Jett said. "Shit."

"It's the Pack," I shouted. There could be no doubt. My wolf eyes flared; a red haze seeped into my vision. This was bad. This was very bad.

"There's no time," I said, all hope leaching out of me. "You have to run. If they find you here..."

But Jett was already on her feet. I strained to see what was happening. From my vantage point and the few inches of clearance under the wall, I saw her booted feet begin to run. Then, she slid to a stop.

"Hey! You!" Oh, God. It was Lowell. With a high, bright moon at his back, Lowell's shadow fell across Jett. He'd come alone, but it wouldn't matter. He was only a beta, but he was still ten times stronger than Jett, at least. She planted her feet wide and aimed her weapon at him. Her bullet would be no match for his shifter speed. She fired anyway. I couldn't see if she'd hit him.

Lowell muttered something unintelligible and lurched forward, his gait all wrong. She'd hit him. Holy fuck, she'd hit him. How in the hell had she been fast enough to get a shot off? He dropped to his knees, blood pouring from a wound in his shoulder.

Fuck. It would only be enough to stun him for a moment. To kill him, she'd have to hit him in the frontal lobe at close range. Even then, it might not have been enough.

Lowell clutched the wound on his chest. His eyes went from red to pale yellow. Then, he fell forward face first and started to twitch. He wasn't dead, but something was wrong. Shifters don't go down like that from gunshots to the shoulder.

More shuffling. Jett was on the move, but I couldn't see her. Further away, something worse was coming. I caught their scent moving fast. There was no time. The Pack was on its way.

Metal scraped at the door. Keys jangled then dropped to the ground. Jett swore. Then, the cell door swung wide and she stepped inside.

"Come on," she said. "We're out of time."

"What are you doing? Jesus! You gotta get out of here."

Jett held a ring of keys in her hand. She stood before me, chest heaving.

"Lowell!" A shout filled the air. "You back there, man?" It was Henny and he wasn't alone.

Jett tossed the keys to me. "Hurry up if you want me to help you."

"Help me? Woman, have you lost your damn mind? They're going to tear you up!"

"Then you better get moving."

With shaking fingers, I unlocked the dragonsteel chains. They fell to the ground. The constant burn I'd felt around my ankles and wrists stopped at once. The relief of it nearly drove me to the ground. Jett's hand on my arm made me stop.

"Come on!" she said. "We've got to move."

I rose slowly and took two steps forward. Then, it was as if a sledgehammer hit me in the chest.

Stop! You will not move!

The voice inside my head drove out all reason. It was him. It was the Alpha. He was moving fast. My body wanted to obey; my mind was chaos.

"Gunnar!" Jett shook me.

"No," I said, clamping my hands over my ears. We wouldn't be fast enough. He would catch us. He would make me submit. Too strong. Too many. It was over.

"I can't," I said. "I won't. You have to do it. Now." I took Jett's hand and pulled the gun up, centering it on my forehead. "Pull the trigger. Don't let them turn me."

Jett locked eyes with me. Hers burned with fury. Her breasts heaved with measured breaths. Her fingers trembled on the trigger.

"Now!" I pleaded as the Pack drew nearer. "You swore it."

A tear fell down Jett's cheeks. She bit her lip then slowly lowered the gun. She held out her hand to me.

"I know another way," she said. "But you've got to run."

"No, do it. For the love of God. Do it! I won't be one of them. I can't. You don't understand."

"I understand more than you realize," she said. She gave me a little half smile that tore at my heart. Then, she turned and ran out of the cell. "Follow me if you want a second chance. Or stay here and be one of them."

NINE

JETT

The guard wasn't dead. He twitched on the ground as his central nervous system short-circuited. It wouldn't last. If I'd shot him in the head, it probably would have killed him, but even then it wouldn't have been instantaneous. There was no help for it now. He couldn't move, but he could still see.

"Turn him!" I yelled to Gunnar. "At least cover his eyes."

Gunnar staggered forward. For a second, I thought he was having his own mental issues. Or, maybe having dragonsteel around him for that long did something to his body. As I started toward the woods and looked back, he recovered. His wolf eyes flashed deadly silver as he stood over the guard. Lowell made a choked sound as he tried to get control of his limbs. He might never be able to again. The neurotoxin lacing my bullet might wear off a bit, but it would never leave his system.

"Why isn't he getting up?" Gunnar shouted.

I went to him, putting a hand on his shoulder. "No time now. They're coming. Even I can feel it."

Gunnar blinked rapidly. His color wasn't good. When he turned to face me, my breath caught. This was the first time I'd seen him full on, not peering under a six-inch gap in some hole in the wall.

Gunnar Cole was the biggest shifter I'd ever seen. That should have alarmed me maybe, but instead, heat coiled through me. I *felt* his heart beating almost as if it were inside my own head. Vera and the others had asked me one question I couldn't answer, until now. As Gunnar stood before me, his muscled chest heaving, glistening with perspiration, I saw the tattoo.

It was just another rumor whispered through the woods. A fairytale we couldn't risk believing. Resistance fighters would rise up and take down the Pack. We would know them by the mark they bore.

Gunnar's eyes rolled back in his head. His knees buckled. I shook him once, hard, and his eyes snapped open again. "Turn him," I said. "So he can't see which way we go."

Gunnar stepped away from me and crouched over Lowell's twitching form. White foam spilled from Lowell's mouth. Gunnar moved with such fierce quickness, it took my breath from me. He curved his arms around Lowell's head and snapped his neck, killing him instantly.

Gunnar turned to me, eyes blazing. "Now he can't see anything at all."

My mouth hanging open, I nodded. "This way," I said. I took a faltering step backward, then turned and ran toward the woods. With each step, a million things ran through my mind. This was crazy. Gunnar clearly wasn't at full strength, but I'd just watched him kill a shifter with his bare hands. He probably hadn't let his own wolf out in weeks, maybe months. I knew enough to understand that could make him unstable. And yet, as shouts reached us from the south side of the camp, none of it mattered. The Pack had arrived. If Gunnar stayed, they would turn him or kill him. I just couldn't let that happen.

"Don't turn on me," I said as Gunnar reached my side. He could easily outrun me even in human form. If he went wolf, he could zip out of here at top speed and all I'd see would be a blur of gray. He didn't though. He stayed beside me.

Gunnar let out a low growl as the shouts from the camp grew louder. "Lowell!"

They hadn't found him yet. The moment they did, we'd be in deeper shit than we already were. Gunnar had been in that camp for weeks. The Pack knew his scent. What in the ever-loving hell was I doing?

"This way," I shouted. We'd reached the camouflaged trapdoor leading to the nearest tunnel. I kicked it aside and launched myself into the ground. Gunnar was close behind. He pushed the leaves and branches back over the hole. The tunnel had been built by shifters, for sure. I had maybe a foot and a half of clearance around me as I started to crawl. As I looked back, Gunnar barely had enough room to move. But move he did.

I clicked on the mini Maglite I had clipped to my shoulder. I knew Gunnar wouldn't need it. His wolf eyes glinted silver. Down and down we went until the tunnel finally forked. At first, the ground shook as footsteps pounded overhead. It had stunned me at first how far vibrations carried through the ground. It felt like our pursuers were right on top of us. But, I knew they were probably fifty yards away and hopefully headed in the other direction.

"Which way?" Gunnar asked. The tunnel branched left and right, or we could go straight ahead. Gunnar wedged himself into the space beside me. My skin prickled. Being this close to him ignited something preternatural in me.

"Right," I said. "About two hundred yards there's an opening. We come up near the riverbank. If it hasn't been moved, there's a kayak. The river rushes fast. We can be miles away in no time."

He hesitated, considering my words. His nostrils flared as he tilted his head and tried to catch the scent of whatever was moving above us. My plan would actually take us closer to the Pack patrols, at least for a few minutes. I was right; I knew I was. And yet, Gunnar didn't trust me. If I had time to be rational, I probably wouldn't have blamed him. But, the thought of the Pack catching him right now made me more afraid for him than I was for myself.

"Gunnar!" I shouted in his face. "We have to move." I didn't wait for his say-so. I dove right and kept on going. Dirt and loose rock showered down as Gunnar made the decision to follow me. Though we moved incredibly fast, time seemed to stand still. I'd never been claustrophobic in the tunnels before. Tonight, I felt like the world was closing in around me.

Thunder shook the ground as groups of heavy footsteps merged above us. This would be the most dangerous part. I looked back. Gunnar's eyes glinted like diamonds in the dark. They lit up the space around him. As he reached forward with his hands, his claws came out.

"No!" I whispered. "Gunnar, no. Stay with me." If he shifted into his wolf now, we'd be well and truly fucked. There was chaos and disorder above us. That was a good sign. It meant they hadn't caught Gunnar's scent.

"Don't give them any help!" I said. Gunnar's eyes dimmed, turning human again. I clicked off the Maglite, pitching us in total darkness. It didn't matter. I knew the way and we were almost there.

As the Pack moved to the east, my heart eased. A blast of heat hit me in the face as the air shifted and we moved toward the surface. The tunnel widened into a small, underground cavern where we could stand. Just above my head was another makeshift trapdoor. I put a hand on it and waited, listening for any sounds of movement above.

Gunnar came to my side. He towered over me and had to crouch so his head wouldn't hit the rocky overhang above. His eyes flashed again as he let his wolf out just enough to listen too.

He gave me a quick nod and I pushed the trapdoor to the side. Tree roots hung in a snarl beside me. I grabbed one to pull myself up. Gunnar's arms came around me. He lifted me as if I weighed nothing. My heart caught and my skin flared hot where he touched me.

As I climbed out of the earth, a blast of fresh air hit me in the face. I squeezed my hips through the hole in the ground and rolled away. Gunnar burst out of the ground beside me. He landed in a crouch, his eyes scanning our surroundings, looking for danger.

"This way," I said, coughing. I needn't have bothered. Even I could hear the rushing river straight ahead. Gunnar took a protective stance in front of me. When he seemed sure we were alone, he nodded again and we moved through the trees.

The Rockcastle River flowed roughly this time of year. We edged our way down to the riverbank. My heart started to beat again when I saw the nose of the kayak peeking out beneath the dead branches I'd used to hide it.

Not waiting for Gunnar, I dragged it out. Though the thing was only built for one, it was of heavy-duty construction. It would hold us both, but it would be a tight fit. Gunnar grabbed the other end and we set in in the water. Without a word, Gunnar climbed in first and held his hand out to me. I would have to sit in his lap. Of course it was the only thing that made sense, but now that I was about to get close to him again, I found it hard to breathe.

"Let's go!" he shouted as the river raged.

Nodding, I took his hand and stepped into the kayak. Gunnar drew his knees up, making space for me. My head spun as I slid between his legs. Every nerve ending in my body sizzled as I pressed my back against the solid wall of Gunnar's chest. He sucked in a hard breath as he lifted the paddle and started to carve it through the water. He was in pain. Adrenaline fueled him, but the effects of months of torture had to have taken their toll.

We moved through the water at dizzying speed. I gripped the sides of the kayak, praying we wouldn't tip. But Gunnar fought the raging current with agile grace. Each stroke of the paddle propelled us away from danger. At this rate, we would cover miles in no time. It should have made me breathe easier, but my body stayed alight with fire.

Gunnar's arms came around me with each stroke. I marveled at his strength and hard-cut muscles. He wasn't like any shifter I'd ever known. He was bigger, mightier, more powerful. The idea that the Pack could still pose a danger to him shocked me. They did though. I could feel the fear in his wildly beating heart. At first, I thought I just felt his pulse pressed against my back. It wasn't that though. It was something else. Something deep inside of me. Again, his heartbeat seemed to become my own.

Finally, the current began to slow and the river widened.

"There!" I shouted. A long beach stretched around a wooded peninsula. The trees were dense here, almost as if no humans had ever touched it. Gunnar shifted his weight and carved the oar through the water. In four strong strokes, he beached us. Sand scraped against the bottom of the kayak and we came to a stop.

A strange sensation came over me. Here, in the kayak, I felt protected, almost as if we existed in some bubble of time. I didn't have to think or act. I could just be. The moment I stepped foot on land, I would have to turn and face this man. What had I done?

Gunnar got out first. He put a steadying hand on my back then reached for me. "Come on," he said. "We've got to get rid of this thing."

I opened my mouth to protest. That kayak had been a hard-won prize. Vera found it a few months ago. We'd used it for supply runs, to scout new territory, and to escape faster than we could on foot when the Pack closed in. But, Gunnar was right. We'd traveled so far away from my encampment and downstream, there was no good way to get it back.

"The less they know about how we're traveling, the better," he said. Swallowing past a dry throat, I nodded. Gunnar threw the paddle into the kayak, waded out into deeper water, then cracked the thing in two with a volatile strength that shocked me. I knew what he was. And yet, his power still startled me. The wreckage of the kayak sank quickly to the bottom of the river.

I didn't wait for him. Instead, I trudged up the beach and headed into the deeper part of the woods. We should be well protected here, but there was always the chance the Pack might venture out this far.

Early spring, and it got bitterly cold here in the Kentucky wilderness. Enough water had splashed up to leave me drenched to the bone. I shivered and drew my arms around me. I pulled the shoulder strap of my small backpack over my head. I'd traveled light. The nine, some walnuts for protein, a lighter, and the Maglite.

"We need to make a fire," I said, my teeth chattering.

"No!" Gunnar came to me, still scanning the tree line. "It's not safe."

The moonlight cast eerie shadows, making the trees seem to come to life. Gnarled branches reached out with crooked fingers, closing in all around.

"We're miles away," I said. "And the Pack's headed in the other direction."

Gunnar seemed unconvinced. He stood with his legs apart in a ready stance. He dropped his head and tilted one ear into the wind. I opened my mouth to protest again but thought the better of it. I knew these woods better than he did. I knew how the Pack moved. But, he could still sense them in ways I never could.

His eyes snapped open and he came to me. "You're freezing," he said. He stood inches away, but his body heat reached me like an aura around him. There was a pull between us I couldn't understand. It frightened me as much as it drew me in.

"I'm f-fine," I said. "I'll make a fire. It'll be all right. I know what I'm doing."

When I turned to walk away, Gunnar took my arm and turned me back. His eyes blazed with hot fury. "You don't."

I erupted. "Are you kidding? I've survived out here a hell of a lot longer than you have. You haven't got the first clue about what I know."

Gunnar's shoulders dropped. That silver wrath still lit his eyes, but his tone softened. "Jett, they're out there. You can't sense them, but I can. Even miles away, they'll smell the smoke. Don't you understand what just happened? Don't you realize what they're capable of?"

Something snapped inside of me. How could he ask me that? He didn't even know me. He didn't know what I'd been through. "Yes," I hissed. "I understand. And I also just saved your ass, so please don't lecture me about..."

A growl ripped from Gunnar's throat. "Saved me? I killed that guard."

"You didn't have to!" I yelled. "He wasn't going to get up. Maybe not ever."

"He saw you," Gunnar yelled back. "Whether he got up or not, he knew what you looked like. Do you get that I'm now the most hunted shifter in Kentucky? There's a bounty on my head. And the Alpha is here. God, I can still feel him. The pull is still there. It's all around us. If he gets closer...*when* he gets closer..."

Gunnar put his hands to his ears. Agony distorted his features and he doubled over.

"Gunnar!" I went to him on instinct. I put a hand on his back. That same heat was there. His skin rippled where I touched him. The instant I did, his breathing grew steadier. He froze then slowly straightened.

He staggered away from me as if my touch burned him. I know it burned me. His expression filled with such desperation, my heart nearly stopped beating.

"Why didn't you do it?" he said, his voice a choked whisper.

"Do what?"

An ancient, rotted log had fallen a few yards away. Gunnar went there and sat. He buried his face in his hands. His shoulders quaked. Slowly, I went to him. I wanted so badly to put a hand on his shoulder. When he looked up at me, his eyes were hollow.

"You made me a promise," he said. "You should have kept it and killed me."

I couldn't hold back. I put a hand on his shoulder. Gunnar flinched from the instant heat I knew we both felt. He didn't stop me as I sat beside him. He was right. I *had* promised to kill him. But now, I knew in my heart that I never could.

TEN

GUNNAR

Jett shivered beside me. She was soaked to the bone wearing a thin t-shirt and her black cargo pants. Winter hadn't completely released its grasp on central Kentucky. It would get below freezing tonight. Her teeth rattled and she drew her legs up, hugging them.

I went to her; acting on instinct, I pulled her against me. Her shivering intensified for a moment before my body heat started to warm her. I wore no shirt, tattered jeans, and had no shoes. I didn't need any of it. I had hot shifter blood running through my veins. But, another kind of heat poured through me as I kept Jett close. She stiffened, reason and propriety making her want to pull away. But, she couldn't deny the undercurrent running between us. I *needed* her close to me. My body craved it. Hers did too.

"L-let me go," she said.

"You're going to freeze to death. It's too dangerous to build a fire. And if you're not planning on keeping your promise and putting me out of my misery, this seems like the best option to keep you from getting hypothermic."

She *should* have killed me. Hell, I'd begged her to. Even now, I could feel the distant pull of the Pack. They *would* find their way here. Not tonight. Jett was right that they were headed in the other direction. It had been a near miss though. If she knew how close I'd come to just giving over to the pull, she never would have led me to the tunnels.

Jett finally settled against me and her teeth stopped chattering. She felt so good in my arms. Not small or fragile. No. Jett's arms were toned, her waist trim. She kept her back straight and her chin jutted in defiance. This was as hard for her as it was for me. She didn't trust shifters. If she'd come from Birch Haven, I knew why. Just the fleeting thought of any of the Pack trying to force themselves on her made my inner wolf rage. My protective instincts flared so hot it got hard to see straight.

I went somewhere else in my mind for a minute. Before I knew what was happening, Jett had slid off the log and stood before me. She was warm for now, but it wouldn't last long.

"You're not okay," she said. "How long has it been? When did they capture you?"

"I don't know," I said, closing my eyes. She wasn't wrong. My head swam and my stomach bubbled. When I tried to focus on a single point, my vision wavered. I'd been so keyed up during our escape, it was only now that my heartbeat started to slow. I'd been cramped up in that cell for so long I hadn't realized how much strength I'd lost. "What month is it?"

Was it January? That would make two months since they'd

captured me. Two months trapped by four walls and chains that wouldn't let my wolf come out.

Jett squatted down in front of me. She put a light hand on my knee. "It's the first week of April," she said.

Her lips were moving but it felt like I was hearing her on a delay. April. Had she said April? That meant it had been almost six months since I'd been taken to Camp Hell. Six months. It was impossible. I hadn't shifted in six months?

"Gunnar," she said. "You don't look well."

I put a hand out to steady myself. My whole body began to quake. "April," I repeated. "That can't be right."

"How long, Gunnar?" she asked again.

Shaking my head, I tried to rise. I took a step forward then faltered to the side. Jett tried to catch me. She was too small. I took us both down, landing hard on the ground. She got to her knees and put a hand on my cheek. "How long?" she whispered.

"Six months." I choked the words out. "I think it's been almost six months."

"Can you...I mean...how?"

I met her eyes. Hers were wide with fear. My vision went white. I had trouble focusing. "Jett," I said. "I have to...I can't..."

"Gunnar, look at me." She held my face in her hands. "You have to shift. You have to let your wolf out. Is that what you need?"

"It's too dangerous," I said. "They can track me."

"They are miles away. You're not thinking straight. Look, I don't know how this works. But, are you sure you're sensing them properly? If you haven't been in your wolf in that long, how do you know if you're instincts aren't, I don't know, haywire?"

Haywire. That's exactly what everything felt like. She was right. God help us both, she was right.

"So shift," she said. "Maybe it'll help you, uh, hit the reset button."

I smiled. It was an odd way to put it, but it made a certain degree of sense. I tried to hold it together, but it wasn't going to work. The urge to shift burned as strong in my lungs as the need to breathe. I couldn't keep this up.

Jett sensed it and let go of me. She rose and took a few gingerly steps backward. "It's okay," she said. She grabbed her pack off the ground and slid her gun out of it, holding it pointed down and away from me. That was another conversation we needed to have. With what happened to Lowell, that thing clearly wasn't loaded with normal bullets.

"I can take care of myself," she said even as her teeth started to chatter again.

"I just need a few minutes, maybe," I said as the hunger began to rise. My whole body trembled with it. My wolf wanted to tear out of me. "Stay here," I said. "If anything that isn't me tries to come through the clearing, shoot it."

Jett smiled. "So you don't want me to shoot you anymore?"

She meant it as a joke, but her smile faded quickly. Before I could answer, she turned and walked toward the water. With Jett's back turned, I slid out of my jeans. Filthy as they were, no sense in ruining them as I didn't have another pair. My wolf rumbled. I dropped to all fours, eyes on Jett's back.

I wanted her. More than I wanted to shift, I wanted her. As I reached out, my fingers turned to claws. The shift shuddered through me. It felt like the first time. My limbs were awkward. My muscles tore and bones reknit in searing agony. It wasn't the seamless change that I'd honed since adolescence. This was ungainly torture. A growl tore from my throat and my fangs cut through my flesh.

Then the world went still. My pulse thundered through me, driving heated blood from the tips of my ears to the pads of my paws. I was the wolf. The wolf was me. Strength that had been torn from me flooded through me once again. A blue moon rose, reflecting off the river before me.

I saw Jett standing in silhouette. My ears pricked at the soft sound of her heated breath. She would shiver again soon. She would need me. My need for her might take hold. For now, I needed to run. Jett turned. Her chin trembled as she stood with her back straight, her hands folded in front of her.

She was afraid of me. She'd never seen a wolf like me before. The wolves of Birch Haven were smaller, weaker. They were betas. The Alpha kept them far away from the women he'd brought there so the lesser shifters would be easier to control.

I was no beta. I was born to be an Alpha, to claim a rightful pack and a mate. Had I been born in another century or another place, I could have taken it. But I was born here, in Kentucky where a ruthless *Tyrannus Alpha* kept all the shifters under his control. Or he would, if I ever let him catch me.

A howl ripped out of me with enough power to blow Jett's hair back. The sound rippled through her and I felt her pulse quicken. It meant something. It meant everything. But, for now, I needed something else more.

Turning, I stretched my legs. With each step, strength poured back into them. I sprang up on my haunches and ran up the hill to the deeper part of the woods. My claws ripped into the ground, propelling me forward with each step. My senses sharpened. The scent of wet earth, bark, grass, blood and prey filled my lungs. I would hunt. I would feed. I would reclaim who I was.

I don't know how long I stayed away. An hour. Maybe two. In the back of my mind, I thought of Jett standing by the water's edge. The urge to keep on running all the way to the border pulled at me. It would be so foolish. The heaviest concentration of Pack patrols would be there. And I knew they were looking for me.

I tore into the flesh of a snow hare that had the ill luck to cross my path. I would need something bigger soon. For now, just the thrill of the hunt helped restore my soul. I howled at the moon once more.

Then, another heartbeat filled my senses. Not Jett. It was something dangerous. I crouched low, baring my teeth. Part of me hoped the Pack would just come. I welcomed the fight. It was part of my nature too. No sooner had I thought it when the pull started low in my belly. My pulse quickened and my vision wavered.

No. No. Not this. Not now. I heard voices in the distance. At first, I thought they were just beyond a small ridge on the other end of the peninsula. Then, slowly I knew they were coming from inside my own head.

Sir, he's close. He's been in dragonsteel for months. He won't be able to stay out in the open for very long and he's too far away from the rest of his people.

You don't know where the rest of his people are. He had help. Gunnar can't shoot bullets from his eyeballs. Did I imagine the gunshot wound on the guard?

If they were close, they would have found him by now. He's alone. He's weak.

With all due respect, sir. I know Gunnar better than anyone. Let me take some men south. We'll bring him back. I won't let you down.

You said he grew close to the other men here. I trust you'll do what needs to be done with them.

Yes, sir. We'll increase the interrogations with the prisoners we still have. If they know anything, we'll know it too in a matter of days. Or less.

My heart felt like it might explode. The voices were inside my *head*. It meant the Pack was far closer than Jett or I thought. The Alpha was talking to Maestro. Maestro told him he knew me better than anyone. For those wolves under Pack control, God help me, he was right.

It would be so much easier if I just went to them. No more fighting. No more pain. I took a faltering step forward, then another. Soon, I was running again.

ELEVEN

GUNNAR

Jett was still by the water's edge. She spun around as she sensed my approach. I took slow, measured steps, letting my paws sink into the sand. Then, I froze, waiting for her. She bit her bottom lip, hesitating. Then, she came to me. I nuzzled her leg. She reached for me. With shaking fingers, she ran her hand over my head, curving them around my ear. Her fingers sank into my soft fur and her breath caught. I'd never let anyone touch me this way. Not when I was in my wolf. I let out a sharp whine then stepped away.

Jett's breath caught. She held her hand out where she'd touched me, frozen. I turned and loped up the hill to the deeper part of the woods. I wanted nothing more than to stay in my wolf and run until my legs gave out. But, the longer I took to shift, the easier it would be for the Pack to find me. If I could hear them in the distance, soon they'd be able to hear me.

I let out a breath and took a single step. For an instant, I didn't think the shift would come. It had been so long since I had to think about how to do it, I thought I'd lost my way. But, then my claws retracted and my fingers stretched out before me.

There was movement in the trees behind me as Jett made her way up from the beach. I grabbed my jeans and pulled them back on, buttoning them just as Jett approached. I turned to her.

"It's okay," I said. "I'm okay. Better anyway."

"You look better," she said, breathless. She grew bold. She came up to me and lifted her fingers to my face. "Your hair," she said. "It's almost gold. It was darker before. And your eyes are clearer too. They're blue!"

It was as if I'd been viewing the world through a darkened film for weeks. Now, that had been peeled away, revealing bright, vibrant colors. I saw Jett in a different light as well. I'd thought her skin pale. Instead, she had an almost olive complexion. I caught her hand, circling my fingers around her wrist. My pulse quickened and hers did too.

Letting my wolf out cleared my head, but it also made my baser instincts flare even hotter. Jett. This woman. She meant something. I stepped closer to her, keeping her wrist in my hand. She didn't pull away. A pulse flickered near her throat. Her breasts pebbled beneath the thin cotton of her black t-shirt. What I wouldn't give to slide my hand beneath the fabric and feel her skin warm beneath mine.

"Gunnar," she said, her voice catching. "What happened out there? I heard you...howl."

"It's the Pack," I said simply. "The Alpha himself. We're not going to be safe out here forever."

"Is there somewhere else we can go?" Jett looked at me with those wide, dark eyes, blinking wildly. It seemed like such an innocent question, but experience made me cautious. Though my heart didn't want to let me believe it, I still didn't know who she was or where she came from. Every instinct in me told me what she was to me, but I couldn't let the words form in my mind. I knew what Liam, Payne, and Mac would say. I couldn't trust her. Not yet. Her appearance at Camp Hell was too damn convenient. Just when Maestro had given up and was about to turn me over to the Pack she showed up.

"Gunnar?" she said, sensing a shift in my mood. Dammit, all of this could be part of the Alpha's plan. Get me to tell her where the rest of my men were hiding. Bring down the Mammoth Forest wolves once and for all.

"I can't," I said, finally letting go of her. "I'm sorry. I can't take you back with me. Not yet."

She shook her head as if she were trying to clear it. She let out a little laugh and brought her arms up, crossing them in front of her. It was a defensive posture and I'd seen her do it a lot. "I suppose you think I'm going to just lead you right to *my* camp," she said.

Her words struck me like a blow to the chest. Of course she had the same fears about trusting me as I did her.

"I'm not stopping you," I said. "Go if you want." It was a bluff. In this cold, she'd never make it through the night. And I would *never* let her leave without me. If the Pack found her...I couldn't even complete the thought before a protective growl erupted from some deep place inside of me. Jett jumped, startled by the sound.

"So you can just follow my trail? I don't think so. I'm staying right here until I know it's safe. Or safer."

I smiled. "Well, then we're at an impasse. You don't trust me to take me back to your hideout. I don't trust you to take me back to mine. Of the two of us, I'm the only one who's kept my promises. I told you what I knew about Birch Haven. You think that wasn't a risk?"

Her mouth dropped open, then comically snapped shut. I had her speechless. I think that might have been a first. I took a step toward her. She took one back.

"So why don't *you* tell me about Birch Haven? Tell me who you really are."

She started to pace. "Jett. I told you my name is Jett. Jett Magrum."

"And you escaped from Birch Haven," I said. She whirled on me.

"I never said that."

"You didn't have to. You knew too much about it to have been on the outside. People on the outside thought it was a nice private college. You probably got a scholarship there that was too good to be true. Then, you found out what it really was. So what I want to know is how. How did you escape? You had to have help. From who?"

Her arms went up again, crossing herself. "And if I tell you that, I put them at risk."

"From who? What do I need to do to convince you I'm not part of the Pack? You saw me *kill* one of them. And about that." I went to her. She had her nine holstered at her hip. She gasped as I reached for it. I didn't disarm her, but I caught her wrists with one hand and ran my fingers over the stock of the gun with the other.

"Those aren't regular bullets. What are they? Where did you get them?"

We were so close. I only meant to examine the gun. But now I stood with my chest pressed against Jett's. The scent of her hair filled my nostrils. Her rapid pulse quickened mine. Her rock hard nipples against my skin did me in. My knees went weak and my vision clouded.

Mine. Mine!

I froze. Jett's pupils widened and a tiny bead of sweat formed on her upper lip as she brought her chin up and up. It was her move I knew, not mine. When she made it, the earth seemed to shift out of orbit for a moment.

Jett tilted her face toward mine. I took one breath, then another. Then, I leaned in and kissed her. A tiny groan escaped her lips as she sank into it. Her little tongue darted out and I let go of her wrists. Jett slid her arms up, pressing her palms against my chest. I looped an arm around her waist and pulled her to me.

Heat. Light. Electricity. My blood sizzled and my nerve endings lit with fire. Though I couldn't be sure yet if she was working for the Pack, one thing was clear. She was mine. There could be no doubt.

TWELVE

JETT

I was hollow, hungry, aching for something. Only until this moment, I'd never realized it. The instant Gunnar's lips touched mine, everything else washed away. There was just the two of us. This time. This kiss. This heat.

A wave rose up and carried me with it. I'd been struggling against the current for so long, now that I let go and let it take me everything clicked into place. A moment ago, I had been freezing. Now, Gunnar's warmth spread through me. We fit.

Every cell in my body seemed to align and send a single message shooting to both my brain and my core. Him. This man. Gunnar. My need for him built with such force my knees buckled. Desire spooled through me, settling in my core. I was wet, throbbing, breathless.

Gunnar broke away first. His wolf eyes flashed bright silver. His lips parted and the tips of his fangs grew. It was startling, dangerous, and dead sexy.

"Jett," he gasped. He seemed as dazed as I was at the hunger rising between us.

No. I can't have this. He's a shifter. He's dangerous. If the Pack...no...*when* the Pack finally caught up to him, they would turn him into the thing I'd been running from for more than three years.

"Jett," he said again, reaching for me. Shock made his eyes widen, going from silver back to blue. Whatever happened inside of me, he was having an even harder time processing it. I wanted to reach for him. My eyes snapped to the bulge in his jeans. I ached for him. My sex throbbed, wanting so badly to be filled.

I shook my head then brought my hands up, smashing them against my temples as if I could drive the desire out of me. I knew I couldn't. On a preternatural level, I knew I never could again.

"I can't," I said, panting. "Gunnar..."

He caught my arm, his eyes still wide and desperate. "I wouldn't hurt you. Do you understand that? I'm not like them. Birch Haven...that's not what I am. And I'm not alone. There are plenty of other shifters, Alphas like me who refuse to live that way."

We stood frozen, connected to each other by our eyes and the searing heat of his fingers on my arm. My heart beat wildly then began to slow. He was doing something to me. For days, I'd pretended he wasn't. But, somehow Gunnar's heart beat with mine.

Slowly, he lifted his fingers from my arm and stepped back. We both needed space and air. Gunnar scanned the trees, his eyes darting left and right. He sucked in a great breath and tilted his head toward the north.

"Can you sense them?" I asked.

When he opened his eyes, I saw his wolf for a second, then he went calm. "Yes," he answered simply. "They aren't close, but they're out there. They're not going to stop until they find me."

He tore a hand through his hair then trudged back up the embankment. He found the rotted log and sat on it. I went to him. I wasn't ready to sit beside him or get close to him yet. My rocketing heart steadied. I felt more like myself. I needed to think straight.

"What are we?" The question just flew out of me. This was uncharted territory for me. I understood the Pack as well as any non-shifter could. They hunted. They took human women for forced mates. The Alpha controlled Pack members absolutely then tortured and killed any who tried to break free. Gunnar was completely different.

Gunnar lifted his head slowly and smiled. "That's the million dollar question, Jett. I only know what I am. You're new to me."

His words came out uneven and halting, like he was holding something back. "I think we're safe here for now. Tomorrow, we're going to have to figure out what to do. I have people waiting for me. People I care about. They're not going to understand about you."

Gunnar raised a thick brow and scratched his chin. "I think that's an understatement. I'll do what I can to help you get back to them."

I don't know what made me do it. Hell, I didn't know why I did anything where Gunnar was concerned now. When this started, it was about a promise to a friend. Now, it was something so much more. I sat beside him and pulled the faded photograph out of my pocket.

"Jasmine," I said. "Did I tell you her name?"

"You did," he said. He took the picture from me, careful not to let our fingers touch.

"There were twelve us who escaped from Birch Haven. One of the shifters helped us. He was maybe like you, I think. I mean...not an Alpha. He wasn't big like you. But, he knew what was happening to the women there was wrong. Anyway, he got us out. His name was Bates. He's dead because of it. He helped us on the outside for a while. Brought us food, told us where to hide to avoid the Pack. Then, about a year after we got away, he told us my friend Jade's sister had been brought to Birch Haven."

"God," Gunnar sighed. "I'm so sorry. What happened to Bates?"

"He was good, but eventually, the Pack figured out he was helping us. They followed him. He was at our camp one night and sensed them coming. We had to...he begged us to..."

"You killed him," Gunnar finished for me. "Just like I made you promise to do to me. He would have rather died than let the Pack control him anymore or find the rest of you."

Now that I'd started talking, everything seemed to rush out of me. The cautious part of my heart beat out a warning. I knew so little about this man. What I did know should have been enough to make me shoot him just like he'd asked me to.

"Jade was the closest thing to a sister I ever had. She was my roommate when we first got to Birch Haven. She came from a worse background than I did. She and her little sister had been in foster care. It killed her to leave Jasmine but she thought Birch Haven would give her a chance to make something of herself so the two of them would have something, you know? It's all she talked about."

Gunnar reached for me. "What happened to you? I mean, before."

I bit the inside of my cheek. My skin warmed where Gunnar touched me. I wanted so much more. I hadn't thought about the "before" part of my life in so long, much less talked about it. "My father was a shifter. My mother was human. They were forced together. I didn't realize that at the time. It was only after Birch Haven that I fully understood what the Pack really does. He wasn't around much. I only have fleeting memories of him. My mother told me he died. She said he was killed in action. The army or something. I know now that was a lie. Hal Magrum was killed in service to the Pack. It was my mom's idea to send me to Birch Haven. We had no money. I got a scholarship. She was...unhappy. She was a disappointment to my father and a failure to the Pack. When she had me there were complications. She couldn't have any more kids. So..."

"So she wasn't useful to them anymore. I'm so sorry that happened to you."

"But you left," I said. "How? Why?"

Gunnar dropped his head. He wouldn't look at me at first. Whatever his answer, I knew instinctively he was ashamed of it. My heart fluttered with all the possibilities. What exactly had he done for the Pack before he broke away?

"I was young," he said. "I got recruited at sixteen. I was to be a soldier for the Alpha. They sent me to a training camp along with three other guys from my neighborhood. They were good. I was better."

Gunnar let go of me. He rose and walked toward a tall, gnarled oak tree. Placing his palm flat against it, he seemed to need the support to get the rest of his words out. I wanted desperately to go to him. My need for his touch burned through me. I stayed still.

"I was a star," he said bitterly. "Faster. Stronger. No matter what it was. I could hunt anything. Fell *anything*. When the Pack officers tried to break me down, they couldn't. I was going to make my own father proud. God, I didn't even know him. Never met him. He was dead before I was born. My mother told me he was one of the Alpha's top generals twenty years ago. Anson Cole."

"What happened?" I asked.

Gunnar didn't look at me. He stared straight ahead. "I was too good too fast. Made the others recruits look bad. One of them, Sean Sutter. He was one of the neighborhood friends I enlisted with. He started turning the others against me. They planted literature in my bunk. Seditious shit against the Alpha. Sabotaged me with the officers and made them think I was thinking of rebelling. So, one day, one of the generals came to question me. He was so strong. The pull he had was almost overwhelming. It scared me. After he interrogated me, I overheard him talking to the officers. He told them there was no hope for me that I was too rebellious. They were going to kill me. So, I escaped. And the further I got away from the Pack's influence, the more I was able to clear my head and see them for what they really were. You could say Sutter and the others did me a favor."

"That's when you found the other resistance fighters?" It just popped out. I'd been so riveted by Gunnar's story I didn't think about my choice of words. He turned on me though, eyes flashing. He crossed the distance between us in two powerful strides and grabbed me by the wrists, pulling me to my feet.

"Am I an idiot?" he said. It didn't seem like he was talking to me. "They're good. God. They're so good. I thought Maestro was the best there was. But this...you...you make me want to tell you things. You make me want to trust you. What I just told you, about Sean Sutter, I haven't uttered his name, told anyone about him in all these years."

My heartbeat quickened, feeling like it slammed against my ribcage. I couldn't breathe. Gunnar's grip was so tight. He terrified me at the same time he drew me in.

"I'm *not* working for the Pack," I said. "That isn't who I am. Everything I told you about myself is true."

He loosened his grip and I snapped my arms away from him. Sweat trickled between my shoulderblades. I gathered my hair in one hand and turned my back to him, exposing the nape of my neck.

"See?" I said. "No mark." Gunnar let out an almost imperceptible groan. The sensitive flesh at the base of my neck flared hot. No, I hadn't been marked by a wolf, but in that instant, I desperately wanted to be. Dropping my hair, I whirled around to face him.

Gunnar's wolf eyes flared. His lips quivered and I saw his fangs had dropped again. Oh, yes, I wanted him. It scared me to think how badly. He said he wasn't with them. But, how could I know for sure? Is this what happened to Melanie? The wolf who marked her was stronger, sure, but she said herself she hadn't put up a fight. She'd wanted to, but it was if her body wasn't her own. He controlled it even before he marked her.

"So you don't trust me, and I don't trust you," I said, moving further away from him. "And yet, here we both are. You're stronger and faster than I could ever be, but that doesn't mean I can't defend myself." I pulled my gun out of my pack and leveled it at him. Inside, I trembled, but somehow I kept my aim steady and straight at Gunnar's heart.

"You can't hurt me unless I allow it," he said, but his tone was more defeatist than threatening. I kept my hands steady, my finger on the trigger. This was a military-issued Sig Sauer. There was no safety, nothing to cock. Just point and shoot.

Something changed about him. It was barely perceptible, but he swayed to the side. His silver wolf eyes slowly faded, turning back to their human, pale blue.

"I am *not* working for the Pack."

"You left Lowell alive," he said. "Is that what they told you to do?"

"Lowell. The guard? I could have killed *you* Gunnar. I didn't."

"Right. Better to keep me alive so I can slip up. Tell you things. Betray my friends."

His color wasn't good. He'd seemed so much better after he shifted. Now, whatever benefit he'd taken from that was wearing off. God, what had they done to him? I kept the gun steady. Maybe he would trust me sooner if I lowered it, but he was still a shifter. He had twenty times the strength and speed that I did. Probably more.

Gunnar's eyes rolled in the back of his head and he swayed to the side. He dropped to his knees with the grace of a falling tree. His heartbeat slowed. I could feel it thumping inside of me, taking my breath away.

"Gunnar!" I shouted. Still, I kept the gun aimed at him. But, I took a cautious step toward him. The wind picked up again.

"Run," he said, his voice a choked whisper. "Jett, run!"

THIRTEEN

JETT

A black shadow moved across the ground. My senses weren't sharp like Gunnar's were. I couldn't sort out the sight from the sound. The woods echoed with a menacing growl. First Gunnar's, then someone else.

A hulking form burst through the trees and skidded to a stop right in front of me. It was an enormous black wolf, its yellow eyes narrowed, his lips curled, revealing glistening fangs.

Gunnar crawled forward, trying to put his body between me and the wolf's. He seemed familiar somehow. I knew him. He snapped his jaw shut and took a slow step toward me, his tail up and his back arched.

My legs shook, but I kept my arms steady and my weapon aimed straight at him. Gunnar made a sound. He was trying to move but couldn't seem to make his legs work. It was the Pack. They were trying to control him. I chanced a desperate glance at

Gunnar. He begged me with his eyes. The wolf let out a fierce growl and came at me.

There was just a moment, not even the span of a heartbeat, but the black wolf's eyes changed, going from yellow to red. It gave me the only chance I would ever get.

I squeezed the trigger.

My shot echoed off the trees but found its mark. The black wolf let out a strangled cry and lunged for me. In the same instant, Gunnar shifted. He did it with such remarkable speed, going from man to wolf in less time than it took me to blink.

He went for the black wolf, but he was already dead. My shot had taken him straight through the heart. Adrenaline and the last spark of nerves propelled him forward. Gunnar's teeth sank into his back. With a mighty snap of his head, Gunnar threw him against a tree. His limp, lifeless body fell to the ground with a sickening thud.

My heart jackhammering in my chest, I slid my gun in my belt holster and went to the dead wolf. In death, he was already shifting back. Blood poured from the wound in his chest.

He was young. Just a kid, really. He had matted black hair and smooth, rosy cheeks that probably didn't need a daily shave yet. My heart broke for him. He would have killed me, but those blood-red eyes told me everything I needed to know. This kid had been controlled by the Pack. His mind and body weren't his own.

"Are you all right?" Gunnar said, gasping. He rose to his feet. He came to me, running his hands over my arms, my back, pressing a palm against my head. He was looking for wounds that weren't there.

"He never touched me," I said. "I'm all right. It's you I'm worried about."

Gunnar's color was normal again. His wolf eyes receded.

"We're not safe here," I said. Gunnar knew it too, but the presence of this Pack wolf affected him far more than it did me. Whoever controlled this kid was still nearby. Gunnar could be next.

Nodding, he rose to his full height. My eyes traveled up and up. Fresh from his shift, his pants had torn and fallen off. He stood before me naked, glistening with sweat. Every inch of him was chiseled perfection from the rippling cut of his chest and biceps, to his solid quads and the perfect, muscled curve of his ass. I couldn't help myself. My eyes were drawn to his manhood. His cock swung huge and heavy.

Gunnar didn't meet my eyes. He turned and grabbed his torn jeans and pulled them back on. They covered all the important parts, but one more shift like that and they'd shred to pieces.

I made a decision. The Pack was close. Even if I couldn't sense it myself, I could see it in Gunnar's eyes. He was scared.

A few moments ago, Gunnar didn't know if he could trust me. I still didn't know if I could trust him. But, if we were both going to survive, one of us had to take a chance.

"Come on," I said, holding my hand out to him. "I know a place," I said, my throat running dry. "We'll be safe there."

Swallowing hard, he took my hand and nodded. We would take a leap of faith together.

FOURTEEN

GUNNAR

The Pack was close. Closer than I was willing to tell Jett. But, she moved fast. Her strength amazed me. Her fire compelled me. For a brief moment back in the clearing, I had touched the Pack mind just enough to see what was coming. The black wolf had been sent to kill her.

We raced through the woods with me at Jett's side. I had the strongest urge to shift and put her on my back. It would be so much faster that way. But, it would also make it easier for the Pack to find me. They'd already done it once.

Jett took a zig-zag path then stopped in the middle of another clearing. She scanned the trees, trying to get her bearings. I was about to fling her over my shoulder and keep going. We needed to put more distance between the Pack and us.

"Here!" she shouted. She went to a tall poplar. Its bark was blackened from a lightning strike. Jett kicked the ground then leaned over. Smiling with triumph, she pushed back a clump of rotted leaves to reveal another deep hole in the ground. She slid into it and called me. Without hesitation, I followed.

This tunnel was narrower than the last and newer. Rocks and tree roots tore into my shoulder as I followed her. After a few yards, we reached a fork. Jett went left. The tunnel expanded here, making it easier for me to get through.

I was impressed. This system was vast. Of course, it was nothing like the miles of underground caverns we'd discovered in Mammoth Forest. But, this underground network took us far away from the Pack and made us equally undetectable. There could be no doubt shifters had made these. They were crude, probably clawed out with bare hands and claws. A tremor of fear ran through me. If shifters made them, could the Pack know about them? It made no sense though. Why would they have let me escape through them?

That same flicker of doubt uncoiled inside of me. Maybe the Pack let me escape with Jett so she could gain my trust. I followed her anyway, deciding to trust my heart and instincts instead of my head.

It took hours, but finally, Jett made another sharp turn and clawed her way up. I emerged beside her into the fresh morning air. We were both covered in dirt. To anyone watching from a distance, we had to have looked like underworld creatures crawling up from Hades. Jett dusted off the mud as best she could. On instinct, I reached for her, smoothing clumps of it out of her hair.

She coughed. For a moment, my heart lurched. She had to be okay. She put a hand up in reassurance. I followed her out of the woods. We emerged near a small lake, the water still as glass.

It was early morning, past dawn. The sun was high and bright.

Jett went to the water's edge and cupped her hands. She let the cool liquid run over her face. She bent at the waist and got her hair wet. I went to her, testing it. It was shallow here, but I could see a sharp drop off just a few feet out. I walked past her and dove in. Weeks of mud and sweat sluiced away from my body. It occurred to me that I must have smelled awful to Jett all this time.

I dove deep, touching bottom. It was the freest I'd felt in months, maybe years. In that moment, I didn't care if she was working for the Pack. I think I would have given her anything. I'd told her things I hadn't revealed even to Liam and the rest of the Mammoth Forest wolves. They didn't know about Sean Sutter. They knew his name, but not what he was to me. For a time, we'd been best friends. Sean had been skinny and pale, unsure of himself. I was the one who convinced him to join up and train with the Pack. I covered for him when he couldn't keep up. I thought we would have each other's backs. How wrong I'd been when he drove a knife into mine.

I'd seen the cold look of jealousy and hatred burn in Sutter's eyes. I'll never forget it. He wanted the Pack to kill me. Most of all, he wanted to do it himself. It's a wonder I ever let myself trust anyone again.

I let myself sink, digging my toes into the thick blanket of seaweed. Looking up, the sun shimmered above the waves. I saw Jett's outline as well. She looked for me. Then, she dove after me.

She was like some sea nymph slicking through the water. She didn't see me. The bottom was far too murky for human eyes. I watched her bare feet kick up, her lungs not allowing her to stay under as long as I could. Finally, I pushed off the bottom and came up for air.

Jett was already on the beach trudging through the sand. I swam to her. She turned, almost smiling. She'd stripped down to her black bra and panties. Her nipples cut hard peaks through the fabric. The weight of the water dragged her cotton underwear almost past her hips. Jett's muscle tone was the kind that came from hard work and survival, not yoga or weight machines. With her hair slicked back, I saw her in a new light. Her dark brows slashed straight across her perfect skin.

I rose. Water dripped off my skin. I felt good and clean for the first time in such a long time. If only it were that easy to leave the Pack behind. I went to her.

This close to her, with just that thin bit of fabric shielding her nakedness, my cock grew hard. She ran her hands over her face, pushing the water away.

"You sure you're okay?" she asked. I was about to say the same thing to her.

"Where are we?"

Jett bit her lip. She was still tentative with me but comfortable here. There was a rocky outcropping about a hundred yards away. Some brush had been cleared out and I saw the remnants of a campfire. She'd trusted me enough to bring me back to her encampment. Someday soon, I may have to decide if I could do the same for her.

"Safe for now," she answered. "The Pack doesn't venture this far usually. We're near Carter Hollow."

"Carter Hollow," I said. Jett's eyes widened. "Are there still twelve of you?"

Jett's arms went up, crossing in front of her. I'd learned she did that every time she wanted to guard her words as well. "No," she said. "I told you, Jade died."

"How?"

"A close call," she said. "About a year ago, before we found this place. We have to move around a lot. We've tried to cross the border into Ohio so many times. The Pack always finds us."

"Of course," I said. "Most of the patrol is on border patrol. It's why men like me...Alphas...have a harder time crossing over. And their numbers are growing."

Jett meant to say something else, but she didn't get the chance. My back went stiff and the hair pricked along my spine. We weren't alone. Two women emerged from the woods, each of them holding rifles pointed straight at me.

Jett turned. For a moment, she seemed caught between them and me. Every protective instinct in me flared to life. I couldn't keep my wolf completely in check. Jett put a hand on my chest. Just that simple touch tethered me. If she hadn't done it, I would have shifted on the spot.

"Wait here," she said, through gritted teeth. She grabbed her shirt and pants off the beach and pulled them on. The two women didn't wait. Rifles still drawn, they descended out of the woods shoulder to shoulder.

The taller woman had a shaved head with black stubble covering it. She had a fierce gaze and a broad nose with full mouth drawn into a straight line. She wore a gray tank top and held her rifle with well-muscled arms. Her companion was smaller, thinner with wheat-blonde hair pulled back in a ponytail.

"Vera, wait!" Jett said, calling to the larger of the two women.

Vera didn't stop. She edged in front of the other woman. It was such a slight movement. She probably didn't even realize she'd done it. I recognized it instantly for what it was. These women were human, but that was an Alpha move. She was protecting her mate.

"You move, you die," Vera said to me. She had a hard look for Jett. "You kidding me with this?"

"He's not one of them," Jett said. "And he knows about Jasmine and Birch Haven."

The smaller woman's eyes widened and her lips parted. She dropped her rifle just a little. Vera nudged her shoulder and she raised it again, the hint of a smile going hard again.

"This is Gunnar," Jett said. "He's the one I've been telling you about."

Vera moved fast. I moved faster. She tried to grab Jett by the arm. I got in between them, my blood raging. "You don't touch her," I said. Jett put a hand on my back.

"Stand down, Gunnar," she said. "I know what she wants." Jett moved toward Vera. She turned and pulled her hair to the side. Of course. Vera gave me a hard glare then ran her hand over the nape of Jett's neck.

Vera didn't drop her weapon, but she reached for me this time. Her cold fingers traced the outline of the tattoo on my chest. "You're one of them," she said.

"Them? What do you know about them?" I asked.

She snorted. "I know *they* have made things a hell of a lot harder around here for the rest of us."

"What are you talking about?"

"Every time one of your people stirs shit up, the patrols around here increase. Makes it harder for us to move freely. Harder to get the supplies we need. Harder to live. You heard about the night raids? Innocent people being dragged out of their homes on suspicion of collaborating with you. Some of them disappear. I've even heard neighbors reporting on neighbors just to save their own skin. Everybody's suspicious of everybody in the smaller towns. You think you're playing it safe staying out of the big cities. Everybody's afraid."

My pulse raged. My fists clenched. "You have no idea who I am or what we do." Hell, even admitting that much was more than I'd told the Pack interrogators. If this was a setup, it was a good one.

"Gunnar," Jett said. "This is Vera. And this is Melanie."

"Is that it?" I asked, turning to her. "Is this all that's left of your twelve?"

"Son of a bitch!" Vera raised her weapon again. "What the fuck are you thinking, Jett?"

"I'm thinking about not dying. And I was thinking about helping someone else for a change. 'Cause what we've been doing isn't working."

"I've kept you alive!" Vera shouted. Sweat formed on her upper lip. Her fingers trembled as she gripped the rifle.

Jett stepped between us. I let out a growl that made Vera's color drain. Melanie stepped back. There was something off about her. The moment she saw me, her fear took on a different character than the others. She seemed to be having trouble even moving right. She was terrified, as if she were seeing something other than what was right in front of her. I'd only seen that kind of fear one other time, on my mother after she'd been marked against her will by a different wolf after my father died.

"Shit," I said, leveling my stare at Vera. "You're worried about what I'm going to do? You got a goddamn human tracking device standing right next to you. Her mate decides to come looking, there's no place far enough to hide."

Vera lost it. She took a shot. It ricocheted off the trees behind me. I stood my ground, not even giving her the satisfaction of flinching.

"Enough!" Jett shouted. "Vera, I swear to God if you don't put that thing away, I'm going to let him loose. Gunnar's not the enemy."

"You think he's your friend?" This from Melanie. She had backed away, shaking her head. "You have no idea what he's capable of."

"Fine," Jett said, throwing up her hands. "What is it they say about the enemy of my enemy then? He's had a hundred chances to hurt me. I told you. He knows about Birch Haven. You see his tattoo. You know who he is. We need help."

"Jett saved your ass," Vera said. She lowered her weapon but not her menacing gaze. "You pay her back by following her here? You know the Pack can track you a hell of a lot better than they can track Melanie. You let me worry about her."

I had a million things to say. A keening howl stopped me short.

"Bloody fucking hell!" Vera shouted.

"You have a safe place?" I asked, my voice rising with alarm. Melanie started to cry. She whipped her head in the direction of the howl. Her ponytail swished to the side. The mark at the nape of her neck flamed red.

"Jett," I said. "We're going to run."

"No," she answered. "We have a place."

"Underground?"

A look passed between Vera and Jett. Vera gritted her teeth and rolled her eyes. "Goddammit. Come on!"

As a second howl joined the first, I followed all three women as they ran toward the woods.

FIFTEEN

JETT

Gunnar stayed glued to my side as we hit the hidden cave entrance on the other side of the lake. Vera practically pushed Melanie into it before she turned and trained her gun back on Gunnar. His low growl might have scared anybody else, but I knew Vera better than he did. She would take on even Gunnar to protect Melanie.

"Vera, stop!" I shouted. "We can fight about this later. Gunnar's here now. There's no hiding the cave."

She pursed her lips and let out a snarl that sounded almost wolf-like herself. But, she knew this was no time for a standoff. The howls faded as if they were headed in the other direction, but we needed to get underground now.

Vera stepped to the side. I went first. Gunnar followed. When I turned to look at him, he jolted straight as Vera shoved the barrel of her rifle into his back. His silver wolf eyes glinted and his lip curled. I made a downward gesture with my hand hoping he'd just let it go for now. He clenched one fist but kept walking.

We headed to the downhill to the back of the cave. Melanie and Caroline were already down there. Caroline had one of our LED lanterns on, sending ghostly shadows over the walls.

Gunnar turned on Vera. "Lady, you better put that thing away before somebody gets hurt. You know you can't kill me with it. You're more likely to kill yourself or one of them down here. Be smart."

"Vera!" Melanie got between them, seeing Vera's face drain of all color. She was about to blow up. "Enough. Have you stopped trusting Jett all of a sudden?"

Vera didn't answer. She took a position against the wall. I took it as progress. She'd at least lowered her weapon. Gunnar busied himself exploring the cavern. It was large, roughly two hundred feet across. A natural spring bubbled up in one corner. When it wasn't safe to head topside, that spring saved our lives.

With his wolf eyes flashing, Gunnar felt the walls. "Is this it?" he asked. "No passages?"

"No," I answered. "None that we can get to."

Nodding, he kept feeling the walls. "They're behind here. Probably miles worth. This could be tunneled." He came to the spring and dipped his fingers in. It was a small well, only four feet across. "How deep is it?" he asked.

"We don't know," Melanie answered. "Deep."

"It leads to the lake," he said. It was a statement, not a question.

Vera kept her position on the wall. She shook her head and let out a snort. Gunnar ignored her and felt along the walls again.

"A mine ran through here," Caroline said. She'd been so quiet in the corner, I'm not even sure Gunnar noticed she was there. He turned to her. Before I could intervene, Gunnar went to her, squatting in front of her where she sat on a rock ledge. Her leg twisted beneath her. Gunnar held his hand out.

"Gunnar Cole," he said.

Caroline's eyes flicked to mine. She smiled and shook Gunnar's hand. "Caroline. Or Caro if you're in a hurry."

"Caroline," he repeated. "Can you walk on that?" He gestured toward her leg.

"She manages just fine," Vera barked, pushing herself off the wall. "We *all* manage just fine."

"Vera..." Caroline started.

Vera wouldn't hear it. She stepped between Caroline and Gunnar, putting a hand on his shoulder, she tried to shove him back. She'd have had more luck knocking one of the cave walls down. Again, Gunnar's eyes flashed. He clenched his teeth and slowly rose.

"You're sitting ducks," Gunnar said, his voice dropping low. "All of you. You were worried about leading me here to your hideout? You wouldn't have had to. I scented you from the lake. This cave isn't stable. The passages are closed off because that wall was part of a cave-in. That wall behind the well? That was open. All you're doing is making it easier for the Pack to find you if the patrols ever make it out this far."

"And what reason would they have to come out this far? Huh?" Vera stood her ground. "There's nobody out here. It's just wilderness and a lake nobody ever visits. They can't scent us from out there. You're full of shit."

Gunnar grabbed Vera by the arm, not hard, but enough so she moved. He led her to the spring. "I said I scented you from the lake," he said. "This spring feeds into the lake. I was underwater and I could sense it. You want proof? Go out there. I'll swim it. I can hold my breath and swim faster than any of you. The Pack members can too. You're lucky one of them hasn't surprised you while you slept. It'll happen. Trust me."

"Right," Vera jerked away from him. "Now they will. Because *you* went messing around at the prison camp and drew attention to us." She pointed a finger at me.

"Stop it, Vera," I said. "I'm not going to keep having this same fight with you. You know why I did what I did. I'd do it again."

"And *you*," Vera pointed at Gunnar. "You have no idea what we're capable of. We aren't sitting ducks. You are. Those wolves out there weren't looking for us. They're looking for you."

"Enough!" Melanie shouted. "Vera, dammit. We're on the same side. Look at him!"

Melanie pressed a hand flat against Gunnar's chest, pointing out his wolf's head tattoo.

"He's a shifter," Vera spat the word out as if it burned in her mouth. "They only know how to take. You of all people should know that."

Gunnar's rage simmered off of him. He trembled from it. I knew he was in danger of shifting right there in the middle of the cave. On instinct, I went to him. I put a light hand on his arm. His bicep bulged beneath my touch, but it stilled him too. It was such a subtle gesture, skin on skin. But, the moment I made contact, I felt bound to him all over again. My heartbeat became his, slowing, beating more evenly. My touch *changed* him just as his seemed to do for me.

"I am *not* Pack," he said, staring hard at Vera. "And you have no idea what we are."

"That," Vera said, drawing her shoulders back, "is exactly the problem." She put her arm around Melanie and drew her away. Melanie kept her eyes locked with mine. She understood something Vera didn't. Her gaze slowly dropped to my hand on Gunnar's arm. A tremor went through her and she blinked rapidly.

Gunnar sighed. "I can help you. That's what I'm trying to say. I know you don't trust me. Well, I don't trust you either." He threw up his hands and moved to the mouth of the cave, following the first stabs of sunlight. He put his hand against the cave wall and trained his ears into the wind.

I went to him, feeling Melanie's stare boring into me. I knew she had questions I couldn't answer right now. I only hoped she could at least keep Vera from doing anything rash where Gunnar was concerned. It wasn't safe for any of us out there right now.

Gunnar went outside and I followed. He dropped down to a squat, feeling the ground and sniffing the air. I bit my lip, holding back my questions. Though I didn't hear anything, I could never hope to sense the Pack the way he did. It was a blessing and his curse, I knew.

Finally, Gunnar rose and turned to me. "Give them time," I said. "We've been on our own for a very long time. We've survived."

""Barely," he said. "That girl, Caroline. She can't walk. She can't keep up with you."

"So we're supposed to leave her behind?"

He shook his head. "No. Of course not. I just mean...she needs help."

"We did the best we could. She took a bad fall and broke her leg a while ago. Melanie and I set it. There was no one else. We can't take her into town. We're on watch lists at all the hospitals. We lost two people the last time we tried. The only way we stay safe is off the grid and out of sight."

Gunnar went to me. He put his hands on my shoulders, gripping me hard, as if he thought I might fly away. "There's someone. I know someone who could help her. If I take you to her."

Dark lines of anguish furrowed Gunnar's brow. I knew why. Just like Vera and the rest of us, it was so hard to trust someone new. I put a hand up, cradling his jaw. His skin was so warm. I was still damp from the lake; my hair hung in strings. A shiver went through me and Gunnar put his arms around me. We'd shared a single kiss and I found myself wanting so much more.

"It's not safe for you here," he said, desperation making his voice crack. He was scared, truly scared for me.

"Gunnar, I told you. We've survived."

"But your friend Vera's right. Because of me, they know about you now."

"Lowell's dead," I said.

"He's got a bullet in him that they know I didn't put there." Something flickered in his expression, as if he were going to tell me something but decided to hold it back.

"What are you thinking?"

He let me go and ran a hand hard over his jaw. Bracing his other hand against the bark of the closest oak tree, he scanned the horizon. "They've moved off," he said. "North. I don't know why."

"I don't care why."

Gunnar closed his fist and bumped it lightly against the tree. "You should. You've been hiding. That's not enough."

"We've been doing more than hiding." His tone angered me. I felt like Vera. Gunnar had no idea what I'd been through or survived. I went to him, standing in his line of vision. "You seem to forget I'm the one who busted your ass out of that POW camp, Gunnar. I can come and go without them knowing. And I can hurt them when I need to." I put a hand on my hip holster.

Gunnar paused. For a moment, his eyes clouded over as if he were watching something play out in his mind. Then, he focused on me, sending that little wave of heat straight down to my toes.

"I never asked you how," he said. "Lowell. And that black wolf. How did you do that? You moved faster than they did. You're not a shifter. Your father may have been one, but you're fully human."

I couldn't help myself, I smiled. I opened my mouth to answer, but Vera's sharp shout stopped me cold. "Jett!"

I turned to her. "I wasn't going to..."

"The fuck you weren't. Jesus, Jett. I don't care if this one's Pack. He is what he is. You seem to want to forget that."

"I forget nothing," I said, my voice hissing with rage. "And you are not in charge here."

"Listen," Gunnar said, putting his hands up in surrender. "You don't trust me. I don't blame you. But right now, we're both in a pretty damn precarious position. The Pack's closing in. Vera, is it? You're right. Jett shouldn't have come to Camp Hell for me. It's put you at risk. Unless you've got a damn time machine hidden in that shitty cave, there isn't anything we can do about it but what we've all been doing up until now. Survive. So, here's what's going to happen. I'm going to patrol these woods and the lake. You're going to stay here with your people where they are less likely to sense you."

Vera set her jaw to the side. She started to charge toward Gunnar. "Who the fuck do you think..."

"Vera," I shouted standing in her path. "Shut up! Gunnar's right and you know it. You just can't stand admitting it. So put your pride and your anger away, and focus on the only thing that matters. Keep Melanie underground and out of sight."

Vera froze, her mouth hanging open in mid-sentence. But, to her credit, she finally snapped it shut. I was right. Gunnar was right. And this was no time for chest-thumping. She couldn't resist pointing a finger at Gunnar anyway.

"Fine, we play it your way for now. But you so much as growl in my direction, or do anything that looks like it's Pack controlled...and believe me, I know it when I see it...you're getting a bullet right between your fucking eyes."

Gunnar rounded on her. He took two slow, powerful steps until he was in her face. "Vera, that's the second time someone's promised me that. You damn well better keep it."

He shot me a heated look, then strode into the woods. Every instinct in me told me to go with him. From the moment I locked eyes with him at the prison camp...no...it was even before that. Since I'd first sensed him near me, I felt as if I belonged beside him. Though I wanted to throttle her at the moment, I knew Vera had our best interests at heart. So did I. I just wondered if she was right and my judgment was clouded. There was really only one person who might know for sure.

SIXTEEN

JETT

We reached an uneasy truce in the days that followed. Gunnar hadn't sensed the Pack getting close. He kept his word and patrolled near the lake each night. Vera's anger cooled, but didn't ease. While he patrolled outside, Vera kept watch each night at the mouth of the cave. On the third night, her exhaustion won out and she fell asleep leaning against the cave wall. I couldn't make her trust him, but I could at least keep them separated for now.

I went to her, testing to see how deeply she slept. I put a hand on her shoulder. She grumbled, but didn't wake. With Gunnar out of sight, this was as close as I would get to getting Melanie alone. I left Vera's side and went back into the cavern.

Melanie was waiting for me in the shadows. Caroline had fallen asleep. If things were calmer around here, that would have been cause for great alarm. It still was, but there was nothing I could do about Caroline's health right this second.

Melanie moved the lantern in front of her and gave me a weak smile. "She asleep?"

"For now," I answered. "Gunnar's down at the lake again. We'll know it if he senses anything." Melanie and Vera couldn't be more opposite. Vera was fire and fury. Melanie was cool and sweet. Where one was weak, the other strong. I sat beside Melanie and reached for her hand. "She loves you beyond reason, Mel. And she's scared to death."

"That makes two of us." Melanie's thick lashes fluttered. She drew in a breath and the courage to ask the question I knew she had. "Jett..."

I put up a hand. "I know what it looks like."

"Do you?"

"Gunnar's...different. Do you see that?"

Melanie's gaze traveled to a far-off point. She did this often. I knew it cost her to remember the horrors that happened to her not so very long ago. "He may be different, but what I see is what he wants. Oh, Jett. I've seen that look before. When my wolf...God...even now I can't stop myself from saying that. Even though it's revolting to me. He wasn't mine. But, there was another girl at Birch Haven. She didn't escape with us. Her name was Doreen. She was a shifter's daughter, but her father came from somewhere in Canada. She said real Alphas don't force markings on women. She said there are supposed to be fated mates and that's what her parents were. I think it mattered to her that I understood this marking of mine wasn't...normal."

Fated mates. The phrase thundered through me like a pulse. Fated mates. It held dark mystery and fueled my desire. Fated. Mates.

"You think Gunnar thinks I'm his?"

Melanie smiled. "I think only you know the answer to that. And I'm not here to lecture you. I just want you to be careful. This mark...whether I was fated for my wolf or not...it's a bond I don't know how to break. I can *feel* him sometimes, in here." She put a hand flat between her breasts and the other to her temple. "When he's close, it's like his heartbeat is my heartbeat. I haven't felt it in a very long time. Vera hopes that means he's dead. But, Jett, he isn't. Don't tell Vera I said it, but it's true. And I'm not saying Gunnar isn't one of the good guys. I'm just saying have a care with it."

I hugged her. "I love you, Mel. You know that. I'd die before I did anything that would betray you or the others. Vera knows that too. She's just blinded by fear when it comes to you. I understand that."

"So do I," she whispered. A shadow darkened the cavern as Vera came back. She was awake but bleary-eyed. I let go of Melanie and straightened.

"You've got next watch," she said to Melanie. "We're going to need some firewood."

"It's been three days," I said. "The danger has passed. If the Pack had any idea we were here, they'd have shown themselves."

"I think you're kidding yourself if you think you know why the Pack does anything. You ask me, they're waiting for something."

"For what?" It was Melanie who asked.

"Hell if I know," Vera said. "Reinforcements? Another full moon? You said you shot that guard back at the prison camp. Maybe they pulled the bullet out of him and figured out what's in it. Maybe they're working out a countermeasure. I just know the longer that wolf is down there, the riskier it is for us."

I wanted to argue with her. She made some sense though, as much as I hated to admit it. Sitting tight was only going to work so long as a survival strategy.

"Anyway," she said. "I'll run down and get some firewood. I feel like swinging an ax anyway."

"I'll go," I said. "You stay with Mel and Caro."

Vera shrugged. She was going to argue with me. I could see it in her eyes. But Melanie gave her a look and she backed down. "Suit yourself."

It was the closest I knew I'd get to a peace accord with Vera for now. If we both kept busy working for the good of the group, we'd be fine today.

I can't deny I hoped I'd find Gunnar right away. But, he must have gone deeper into the woods. I took our one machete and hacked away at some branches big enough for kindling. We couldn't risk a big fire, but we'd need something to boil the spring water. If Gunnar's instincts were right, we'd be underground for at least a few more days.

I don't know how much time passed, but I lost myself in the rhythm of chopping and gathering new wood. Hours at least. The sun hung low in the sky and sweat poured off my back.

Humming caught my ear and made my skin prick. I knew instantly that Gunnar was nearby. He had stayed away for most of the last three days, letting the others get used to him being here. At least, that's what I told myself. The simple truth was, I think he was just as unsettled around me as I was him.

Melanie's words tore through me. His heartbeat became my own.

I set my bundle of wood down and followed the sound. I didn think I could sneak up on him, but Gunnar was in a clearing, his back turned toward me. He paced, crunching dry leaves beneath his bare feet. Sweat poured down his strong back and he held his hands on either side of his head.

"Can't. Won't. Get out!" he murmured. My pulse jumped as I realized with growing horror he wasn't talking to himself. Not exactly.

Gunnar thumped the side of his head. "Get out! I won't do it!"

He paced. His shoulders bunched and his skin went from tan to gray and back again. He seemed caught in mid-shift. Terror gripped me as I realized whatever was happening, he wasn't fully in control.

I crouched down so he couldn't see me when he turned. He froze and I froze with him. He stared straight at me but through me, as his silver wolf eyes faded to red.

SEVENTEEN

GUNNAR

Y*ou're fooling yourself, Gunnar. You think you're breaking away from me, but you're only making it that much easier.*

"Oh, yeah?" I put my hands on my temples. "Then why aren't you here right now, motherfucker? The more you tell me I'm losing, the more I know I'm not."

Laughter. His scraggly voice sent goosebumps down my back. I crouched low, scanning through the trees. Dammit, the Alpha *did* sound closer this time. It was an illusion though. It had to be. Why wouldn't he just send the Pack to grab me?

Gunnar, it'll be quick. I promise. Don't you know you were born for this? Why do you think it hurts so much when you fight?

I was on my hands and knees, digging my fingers into the ground. He wanted me to shift. Oh, God. I could feel the command as if it were part of me. Like breathing. I reached out with my right hand. My vision wavered and my nails turned to claws. My heart beat like I hammer. This wasn't me. I wasn't controlling the shift.

"No!" I shouted, rising. My voice echoed off the trees. "Can't. Won't. No!"

I couldn't see. I couldn't breathe. I felt the Pack closing in. They were right beside me. We moved together. No. That couldn't be it. I was safe. They didn't know this place. I couldn't let them see.

No! This time, when I tried to form words, only my wolf's growl came out. He was winning. I was losing. This wasn't me. I stumbled to the ground. He couldn't control me if I wasn't conscious, could he? It was the only thing I could think of. While I still had control of my limbs, I launched myself at the nearest tree, head down.

The world exploded in light and pain, then went mercifully dark.

I floated through the stars, weightless. Something pulled at my middle. A drum beat inside my head. No. Not a drum. It was my heart. Her heart.

"Gunnar!" Her voice opened me up, hitting me in the chest like a beam of light. Then, that beam turned solid. It became a tether. I felt my hands, my feet, my bones. When I moved, *I* willed it this time.

"Gunnar," she said again, softer. Hot rain fell on my cheek. I tried to open my eyes. It wasn't rain at all.

The scent of Jett's hair filled my lungs. She smelled soft and clean from the lake. Agony enveloped me, but I managed to open my eyes. Bright sun. Soft tears. Jett's brown eyes widening in shock. She was solid, warm, real.

"Gunnar?" she said again. She put a hand to her lips and squeezed her eyes shut in relief. Another of her tears hit my forehead.

"Baby," I whispered, reaching for her. I'd never called her that before, but it felt right. She clasped my hand and held it against her breast. Desire flared through me, anchoring me to myself. A wall went up when she touched me. No. It was more like a shield. Far in the distance, I heard the Alpha's voice, but this time I couldn't make out any of the words. He couldn't get through.

"Jett?" I said. I was fully awake now. Pain slammed into me where I'd driven my skull into the oak tree. Maybe that hadn't been the greatest idea I'd ever had.

Jett smoothed the hair out of my eyes. She sat with my head cradled in her lap and her back braced against the tree. "Your eyes," she said, sniffling. "Gunnar, your eyes."

I blinked. My vision blurred for a second, then came sharply into focus. My eyes seemed all right.

"How long?" Jett asked. I struggled to get up. She kept a firm grasp on my hand, but shifted position until we sat facing each other.

It was in me to lie to her or downplay what was really going on. Instinct told me if I didn't come clean, I'd lose her forever. I also knew the truth might bring the same result.

"The night before you busted me out of Camp Hell," I said.

"The Alpha," she said quietly.

"Yes," I answered. "Valent. His name is Able Valent."

"He tried to turn you." Jett sucked in a great breath of air as she braced herself for my answer. She'd trusted me enough to bring me here. I knew she had to be rethinking that now. Anyone would. I owed her honestly. Hell, I owed her my life such as it was.

"Yep," I said. "At least, that's what he wants me to think. I can hear him in my head sometimes. But it's like...he can't close the deal. Or he doesn't want to. He's waiting for something."

Jett wiped the tears beneath her eyes and straightened her back. "Does he know where you are?"

I shook my head. "No. At least, I don't think so."

She sucked in her bottom lip and looked skyward. "You know if Vera finds out about this, she's liable to kill you. She said something. She said maybe the reason the Pack hasn't come yet is because they're waiting for something. Do you think they're waiting for you to turn?"

"Maybe I should let her kill me." My voice went hollow.

"No!" Jett's startled both of us with the ferocity with which she said the word.

"It's safe," I said. "For now. He can't get in. I keep fighting him off."

"You don't think he's holding back just to toy with you?"

It was a good question. I couldn't really come up with a way to explain it to her, except I knew it wasn't true. "I think he's been trying to turn me all along. I keep pushing back. Or at least...he realizes that if he *does* turn me, I won't be much good to him."

"How can you be sure?"

I reached for her, curving a hand around her jaw, I threaded my fingers through her hair. Jett was soft and strong all at once. "You don't want to hear this."

"I think I have to hear it."

My heart thundered inside of me. I knew it bled through to hers. One heartbeat. One pulse. The truth had been staring the both of us in the face for days. Neither of us had dared to give voice to it. Now was the time.

"You," I said. "You're the reason he can't get in."

"Me?"

I took her hand and placed it against my chest where she could feel my heartbeat the strongest. No, that wasn't true. I knew there was another place she could feel it even more. I put my hand on her chest.

Jett let out a hard breath. Her tears welled again. The truth was right there. I knew she could feel it just as much as I could. But, she was afraid. I wanted to tear apart every wolf who had made her believe the worst. The Pack *wasn't* who we were. They did not live the way we were supposed to.

This. This was real. True. Right.

"Gunnar," she said, breathless. "I'm scared."

"I know. I am too. But, I swear to you, I'll never hurt you. I'll never touch you without..."

"I *want* you to touch me. That's what scares me."

I lifted my hand from her and let her go. This had to be her choice. Though I was desperate for her to make it, I would never force it. I would die. I would even give in to the Alpha's subjugation before I laid a finger on this woman she didn't want. And yet, in her was my own salvation. I knew it. I *breathed* it. I'd told her the truth. My connection to Jett was real and strong. It was supposed to make me the Alpha I was born to be.

Jett went up on her knees. We both seemed to hover in midair for one heartbeat, then another. Desire raced through me. She was so close. So sweet. Hunger gripped me, churning my insides. My vision flared bright as my inner wolf came to the surface. She saw it in my eyes, I knew. I could never hide it from her.

"I want..." she said. Then, Jett's own desire washed over her and she was beyond words. I held my hands to my sides, curling them into fists to keep from reaching for her. I wanted to so badly. I wanted to slide my hands around her waist and pull her to me. The slope of her hips, the curve of her round ass, those ample tits with perfect nipples. I wanted to own all of it and give her pleasure unlike anything she'd ever known. I'd make her body sing for me. Spread her open and make her beg for my touch.

All the blood in my body surged straight to my cock. I was rock hard, bursting at the seams. And yet, I found the strength to stay still.

Jett put a tentative hand on my chest. She traced the lines of my tattoo as if she was seeing it for the first time. I dug my fists into my thighs. I would not move. I would not take what she hadn't yet offered. Slowly, I got up off my knees and stood before her. Jett rose with me.

Her eyes flicked to mine. Her pupils widened and her lips parted. The faint, tiny hairs covering her body stood on end as she pulsed with desire. Her nipples peaked beneath her black tank top. It clung to her like a second skin and I could see the outline of her areolas through the fabric. I wanted to tear it from her, tease her with my tongue. My mouth watered as I envisioned it.

She stepped back, her eyes raking over me. I knew what she saw. I stood with every muscle corded, my cock pulsing with need. I watched her with my wolf eyes and to her they would glint silver. She knew exactly what I was.

Jett grew bold. She came to me. I stayed still as a statue as she reached for the button on my jeans. With her eyes locked on mine, she worked the zipper and peeled away the tattered denim. My cock sprang free and Jett gasped at the size of it. Her lips trembled; her body glistened with a thin sheen of sweat.

I moved only to step out of my jeans. Though I wanted to touch her, I didn't. I let her take control. She put both hands flat against my chest and went up on her tiptoes. Tilting her head to one side, she offered me her mouth. I leaned into the kiss but kept my hands at my sides, though it killed me not to embrace her.

Jett groaned as I darted my tongue inside her mouth. She was hot, inviting. I fantasized about how it would feel when she used that mouth on me.

Jett pulled away, gasping, her cheeks flushed. She ran her hands down my biceps, over my hips, then stepped around me. She touched my shoulder, trailed her fingers across my back, cupped my ass, then worked her way back around until she faced me.

"Are you mine?" she asked, cocking her head to the side. It wasn't a tease. I knew she was trying to understand.

"Yes," I said, my voice ragged and raw. Desire clouded my vision, but not my judgment. The Alpha could get in my head. Being with Jett drove him away.

"Fated mates," she said.

I clenched my jaw hard and nodded. "Yes." God, I wanted her so badly. Had I kissed her again, pulled her to me, I knew she would have given in to it. I could *feel* her own lust making her knees weak.

But this was more than just sex. I needed it like the air in my lungs, but I couldn't undo it if we went any further.

"You draw strength from it?" she asked.

I moved. Jett's lips parted and she drew in a breath. Hard as it was...hard as *I* was, I knew this wasn't the right time. She wasn't ready. I reached down and pulled up my jeans. They chafed as I zipped them around my erection.

I went to her finally, circling my hands around her wrists. I kissed each palm. "Yes," I said. "I draw strength from it. Being with my mate...with you...is part of my nature. Submitting to Able Valent isn't."

"What happens if we...if you..."

I finally did kiss her. Though both of our hearts and bodies clamored for more, this would have to be enough for now. At least until I knew I could keep her safe.

"Jett!" Vera's shout cut through the air. I smoothed Jett's hair away from her face.

"You should go," I said. "I'm all right now."

Nodding, she stepped out of my arms, her breasts still heaving with the desire heating her blood.

"Stay with me, Gunnar Cole," she said.

Smiling, I gave her a salute. "I'm not going anywhere." I only hoped it was a promise I could keep.

EIGHTEEN

JETT

I came alive when I met Gunnar. Only, I hadn't realized it at the time. Now, it was as if all the signs in my life finally pointed to one thing. If I had never survived Birch Haven, I wouldn't have met Jade. I wouldn't have made her the promise that led me to that prison camp where I found him. And now, I could *feel* the strength he drew from my presence. His pulse beat alongside my own. It wasn't a trick. It wasn't the Pack. It was me. Only now I had to figure out a way to make Vera and the others accept it. Baby steps.

We settled into a routine over the next few weeks. Spring finally settled as April bled into May. I can't say Vera liked Gunnar yet, but she accepted him for now. In the end, Caroline had tipped the scales in Gunnar's favor. We couldn't stay in the cave anymore. That was clear. It was time to take the tunnels northwest, toward the Illinois border. For some reason, the patrols were lighter there. Tennessee and Ohio were the most dangerous this time of year.

Caroline's leg had gotten worse. I knew she had an infection deep in the bone. For now, it hadn't spread, but we all knew it was only a matter of time. Blessedly, that day wasn't today, but Caroline could no longer bear any weight on her bad leg. When Melanie tried to make a stretcher out of dried vines and branches, Gunnar put a stop to it.

"I'll carry her," he said, facing down Vera.

We were all at the lake, filling what canteens we had. Even that drove Gunnar insane. With his wolf senses, he could scout clean water easily.

"We have managed for years without you," Vera said, bringing up the same argument she'd made for weeks. Now, even Melanie was tired of hearing about it. To his credit, Gunnar didn't take the bait this time. Caroline did.

"Vera, will you shut up? If Gunnar were going to call the Pack down on our heads, he'd have done it by now. If you don't want him knowing about our next hideout, I get it. It's valid. But you've got two choices, either leave me behind or let him carry me. I'll understand either way."

Caroline didn't usually talk like this. It alarmed me more than the swelling in her leg. Gunnar shot me a look. We hadn't said it outright to each other, but if we didn't find medical help for Caroline soon, that leg was eventually going to kill her.

Melanie put a light hand on Vera's back as she stooped to fill up the last of the canteens. When she straightened, she gave me a hard glance and jutted her chin at Gunnar. "So, now you're all against me."

"No one's against you," I said. "For the love of God, Vera. Let's just finish breaking down the camp and get moving. We've stayed here too long as it is."

"Whose fault is that?" Vera muttered as she grabbed the canteens and headed back toward the cave.

"She's trying," Melanie said. Gunnar laughed. Caroline struggled to get to her feet. Agony had etched deep lines in her face. She'd aged years in the last few weeks.

"Let me," Gunnar said, hooking an arm under hers. He shot me a wink as Caroline's shoulders fell with relief. The two of them followed Vera, leaving Melanie and me alone at the water's edge.

"Are you okay?" Melanie asked almost absently as she washed her hands in the water.

"Am I what? Of course," I said. "I mean, as okay as any of the rest of us. I'm just anxious to get out of here. Same as all of you."

"He hasn't marked you," Melanie said. It was a statement, not a question.

I froze as I leaned over to lace up my boot. Melanie had been watching Gunnar and me. Maybe even more closely than Vera.

"Mel," I said. "He hasn't so much as touched me without me instigating it."

"That's good. Because...if you let him...it's forever. You know that."

I know she came from a good place, but I couldn't help that her words got my back up. She didn't know what she was talking about. Gunnar wasn't like the wolf who'd marked her. It wasn't the same at all. Any hint of a comparison felt...blasphemous to me somehow. I held my breath for a beat as I let my misplaced anger fade.

"I know," I said. Melanie was the gentlest person I knew. Because of it, she was sometimes the most cutting. She didn't like to confront people like Vera did. So, when she came at me, I knew it was something she'd been holding on to for a very long time.

"You don't know, Jett. That's what I'm trying to tell you. Vera hasn't figured it out yet, but I have. Gunnar may not be Pack, but he's not entirely free."

My spine stiffened. My need to protect Gunnar flared inside of me. For a moment, I wondered if this was what it was like when his wolf raged within him. It felt feral, dangerous, almost out of place. This was Melanie after all. I took a breath and sat down beside her.

We looked out at the water together. A flock of wood ducks paddled across the surface, a female chased by three larger males. Her sharp quack and a flap of her wings sent them skittering in all directions.

"He's not Pack," I said again. "And I know what I'm doing."

"Do you? I mean really?"

"What happened to you is not remotely like what's going on with Gunnar and me," I said, keeping my tone measured.

"I know that," she said and it surprised me. After everything she'd suffered, that Melanie could look at another shifter and see something other than a monster amazed me. I wondered if she might just be the strongest of all of us.

"He's out there, my wolf," she said. "He's not dead. Vera likes to think so, and most of the time, I just let her. But, I know different. My mark still flares hot sometimes. I can *feel* him in my sleep. He even calls my name."

"You told me that before. But, Mel, it's been years. If he was a danger to you or us, don't you think he'd have shown up by now?"

My pulse hammered inside of me. Melanie stared off into the distance. Her body swayed side to side, giving her a trancelike quality. She was reaching out to him. Horror filled my heart. Then, her eyes snapped open and she looked at me. Wherever she'd gone in those last few seconds, she was fully present now.

"He doesn't care about me anymore," she said. "That's the only reason he hasn't come to drag me back. I don't know why. My guess? He's forced himself on another woman he likes better. And maybe the Alpha doesn't think we pose any kind of threat. I suppose we don't. Not really. But someday, he *will* figure it out. Because Gunner will tell him about us."

Her words stabbed through my heart. These were the kind of things Vera had said from day one. It never occurred to me that Melanie believed it. "Then why?" I asked. "If you were afraid of that, why in the hell didn't you side with Vera and ask him to leave?"

Melanie smiled. "Because he's *not* like the rest of them. Not yet, anyway. And....well...he's yours. I'm still holding out hope that your bond with him will be enough to save the both of you. It might be. I don't know enough about these things. But, you're not going to be strong enough to hold things off with Gunnar forever. He might be; he's a shifter. You're not."

"Why don't you let me worry about that, Mel?" I said. "Vera's rubbing off on you. Come on. Let's get back to the camp and make sure Vera hasn't killed Gunnar yet." I said it with a laugh, trying to lighten the mood. I hoped to my feet but Melanie didn't rise. She just stared up at me, cupping her hand over her eyes to shield them from the sun.

"Jett," she said. "She will kill him. She'll have no choice, maybe."

"What are you talking about?"

"We need Gunnar to help Caroline so we can get out of here. But, after that, he's going to have to leave. Then, you'll have a choice to make."

I squatted back down and faced her. "Are you threatening me?"

"No," she said. "Vera never wanted it to sound like that, and I don't either. It's not your fault. It's fate. I understand that. But, if you really search your heart, you'll know why it has to be this way. You can't be with both of us. If Gunnar marks you like he's supposed to, then you belong with him. Are you going to sit there and lie to my face? Are you going to tell me the Alpha's not already in his head?"

I opened my mouth to argue then clamped it shut. My head swam from the driving beat of my pulse. I couldn't think straight.

Melanie dusted off her ass then finally rose to her feet. "I told you. We love you. I want you with us. But Gunnar's not going to be safe to have around forever. So, decide what you want. Him or us. I will not let him lead the Pack back here."

I forced a smile to try and lighten the air. "It's going to be okay," I said. "You have to trust that I know what I'm doing."

Melanie had a faraway look; her gray eyes misted then flicked back to mine with laser focus. "It will be the same for me some-day. The difference is I already know it. Vera doesn't. I would appreciate it if you didn't say anything to her."

"What do you mean?" My insides felt hollow.

"Someday, Gunnar will pose a threat to the rest of us. And so will I. I'm on borrowed time. I'm ready to do what needs to be done to protect the people I love. Will you?"

She leaned forward and kissed me on the cheek as I stood speechless before her.

NINETEEN

JETT

The plan was to leave at first light. The girls slept in the cave like always. Tonight, I couldn't. Gunnar's slow, steady pulse called to me as he stood by the water's edge.

I went to him. A full moon lit my path.

At first, I couldn't find him. Then, his mournful howl vibrated through my core. His wolf stood tall and majestic on an outcropping of rock on the other side of the lake.

God, he was the most beautiful thing I'd ever seen. His fur was thick and gray with slashes of black around his eyes and across his shoulders. He sat, sniffing the air. The fur near his throat and down his chest gleamed white. He saw me and his silver eyes flashed with magic.

He bounded off the rocks on powerful haunches and ran toward me. He had a smooth, long stride that made him look as if he were running in slow motion. My breath caught as he approached. He stopped then pawed the ground.

I went to him. I had never been this close to him while he was in his wolf. Reaching for him, I buried my hands in the thick downy fur of his neck. Sinking to my knees before him, I pressed my cheek against his flank.

His powerful heart beat steady beneath my touch. My own matched his rhythm. I ached inside when I wasn't near him. But this, this felt good and natural. Gunnar nuzzled against me, lowering his head.

I let him go. Gunnar took two loping steps to the side then arched his back. His fur rippled, the moonlight catching the silver strands. He dropped his head low and his tail went up. I heard a quick pop of bone before his paws stretched out, morphing to hands right before my eyes. Energy crackled around him as he drew on elemental magic. My hair stood on end the way it would in an electrical storm. My heart raced as Gunnar's fur became flesh and he rose tall and steady on two powerful legs.

Gasping, awestruck, I fell back on my ass. Gunnar's slow smile warmed me. He reached for me, taking my hand.

"Come on," he said, his voice not quite human. "It's still gets cold at night."

I knew I should go back to the caves. But Melanie's words had me unsettled. I knew I should say something to Gunnar. Before we moved with the others, he should know what I'd been asked to do.

Could I make that choice? Could I let Gunnar go to save Melanie and the others? Two months ago, it wouldn't have even been a question. Now though? Hot tears sprang to my eyes at the thought of leaving Gunnar behind.

He sensed something. His eyes narrowing with concern, he threaded his fingers through my hair and put a chaste kiss on my cheek. The chill of twilight finally reached me. I shivered. At the same time, I became keenly aware of Gunnar's nakedness in the wake of his shift. I wanted nothing more than to run my hand over the solid curve of his ass and bring him to me. Somehow, I found the strength to keep my hands to myself as Gunnar grabbed his jeans off the beach and put them on.

"You heading back up?" he asked. It was a casual question, but my answer hung heavy in my heart.

"Maybe later," I said. "Right now, I like the air out here better."

Gunnar smiled and headed to the cluster of trees where the beach ended. He liked to sleep under the canopy of poplars and elms. Close enough he could reach the water and mask his scent if he sensed the Pack. And close enough that he could get to the caves if he felt me in distress.

He settled himself, staring up at the stars. He had his arms behind his head and I lay down beside him. He didn't move. He just let me curl up, resting my head on his chest. His strong heartbeat comforted me. This was as intimate as we'd been since that morning in the woods when he let me explore his body but kept still.

"Are you scared?" he asked.

I debated telling him what Melanie said. I didn't want to believe it. She was wrong. Gunnar was an Alpha himself. He wasn't weak like her wolf. He could fight off Able Valent or anyone else who came along. Couldn't he? Of course, I knew I was naive. But, I just wanted things to stay the way they were.

"Are you?"

Gunnar turned to his side. He smoothed my hair back as the moonlight caught his eyes. "Yes," he answered simply.

Again, Melanie's words thundered through me. I should tell him. I should decide now. I couldn't. Vera, Melanie, Caroline and me...we'd been through so much together. Each of us had risked our lives to save the others time and again. We'd lost so much together too. No one would ever understand what I'd been through more than they did. We carried the memories of the other eight women of Birch Haven as well. We were all that was left.

Then there was Gunnar. It should have been an easy choice. He was a shifter, after all. The Pack's most hunted rebel. And yet, here I was lacing my fingers with his and leaning in for another kiss. The Birch Haven women held my story, but Gunnar was starting to hold my heart.

"How is it supposed to be?" I asked. Gunnar's eyes flashed. He knew exactly what I meant. His fingers curved around my neck. A wave of desire coursed through me as he traced an outline at the base of my neck where his Alpha's mark belonged.

"I don't know, exactly," he said. "That's the truth. But, I've seen other wolves and how they are with their mates. Their true mates. They tell me it made them whole. It's a bond that holds no matter how great the distance. But, I've also seen what happens when it's broken."

"How?"

Gunnar dropped my gaze. His face grew hard. "A friend of

mine, Jagger. His human mate was killed by the Pack. He hasn't recovered and I don't know if he ever will. It's made him crazed, wild. And he was among the strongest of us."

A chill ran through me at Gunnar's words. It was almost as if I could feel his pain right along with him. I knew in my heart that a marking would make that even more intense. And yet, I craved it with everything I was.

"You should head back," he said, his voice thick with desire. I wasn't the only one craving something tonight. "We've got a big day tomorrow and you need your sleep."

I touched his face and sat up. Though it tore at me to leave him, I knew he was right. I only hoped I had the strength to do the right thing tomorrow. Whatever that was.

TWENTY

GUNNAR

Tension ran through the group as we left their cave encampment. For my part, I felt relief. The women had stayed too long in one place, and the Pack patrols had reached at least the edge of the woods near the lake. Sure, they hadn't come back since, but even that was cause for concern.

Able was quiet inside my head. Jett was the reason. When I was close to her, my mind felt clear, steady, and strong. She took the lead as we hiked north, staying along the Rockcastle River. I tried to keep my mind blank. With each step we took, I feared the border patrols.

I shifted Caroline's weight on my back. She had no strength in her legs, so I held them around my waist as she gripped my shoulders. She was sicker than she'd let on to the others. The pulse in her right leg was weak and thready. The heat of her infection seared through her jeans where I held her. Without proper medical care, she probably wouldn't survive the month. Even with it, I wondered if it weren't already too late.

Molly would know what to do. I squeezed my eyes shut trying to drive out thoughts of her and the others back in Mammoth Forest. Partly because I didn't fully trust my own mind. Ever since Able Valent invaded it, even thinking about my friends could put them at risk.

"We'll hit the Gold Rock in about three miles," Jett called out. She took point. Sweat poured from her brow and made her tanned skin glisten. Her gray t-shirt clung to her. I dropped my eyes from the outline of her taut nipples beneath the thin fabric. Caroline tightened her grip around my shoulders.

"Keep following the river," Jett said, her eyes catching mine. She adjusted the rifle-strap on her shoulder. Melanie walked directly behind me. Vera brought up the rear, walking backward much of the time. She carried the other rifle. I'd been against it. I thought the weapons would slow them down. Plus, I'd never believed either of them could get a shot off in time if they were ever in range to hit one of the Pack. They moved way too fast. Except, I'd seen Jett do exactly that. Twice. Even with everything we'd shared, she stayed cagey about that. We still had secrets we weren't willing to share.

I gave her a quick nod to let her know I'd caught no scent of the Pack. We read each other's nonverbal cues more and more. Vera would never trust me. If she thought Jett was making decisions based on anything I relayed to her, we would fight every step of the way.

"We should stop to rest for an hour or so," Melanie said. "Caroline could use it. We need to eat."

I opened my mouth to protest but Jett made a quick downward

gesture with her hands. There was something going on between her and Melanie. I'd sensed it yesterday, but Jett hadn't wanted to talk. I let it go. Staying in the wooded areas and away from towns, we'd reached a small clearing. Two fallen trees formed a natural bench. Jett trudged up to the moss-covered hill between them.

"Fine," Vera said. She slung her rifle over her shoulder and reached into Melanie's backpack. She'd packed nuts, berries, and dried venison for the rest of them to eat. The deer had been my contribution, much as Vera hated admitting it. The simple fact was, if it weren't for me, they wouldn't have been able to leave the caves at all.

I put Caroline down as gently as I could. Her ashen color alarmed me. She shot me a quick smile and made her own nonverbal gesture, showing her palm. *I'm all right.* I knew damn well she wouldn't be.

Vera doled out rations. Jett sat a little away from the group on the end of one of the logs. She shot me a wink and patted the space beside her. "You eat," I said, wanting very much to lean down and kiss the top of her head. We refrained from any displays of affection around Vera though. "I'll keep watch."

Vera shot me a hard look. I ignored it. Part of me could respect her ferocious loyalty to the group. As an Alpha, I understood it. She wasn't here to make friends; she was here to protect the others...from me. I touched Jett's shoulder, then stalked the perimeter.

Letting my senses take over, I scanned the woods. It was quiet here, almost eerily so. Two miles to the west, one of the major highways ran through this wilderness. I could hear the distant rumble of semis. Civilization never seemed so close and yet so foreign to me. I wondered if I'd ever be able to walk among regular people again. I wasn't sure I wanted to.

Out of the group's line of sight, I slipped out of my clothes, folding them neatly at the base of a thick oak tree. I let my wolf out. Vera would probably try to shoot me if she saw this, but it didn't matter. She would run out of rations in two or three days. No matter what, I had no intention of letting Jett starve.

Clean air filled my lungs as I chased smaller prey. Within a few minutes, I'd taken two rabbits and three grouses. Anymore and Vera wouldn't be able to carry it. She refused to let me help her, thinking Caroline was enough. She had no idea how strong I really was. None of them did. They'd only ever encountered beta wolves before.

Satisfied that the girls would have enough for a while, I shifted back and tugged on my jeans. I could hear Melanie's lilting laughter in the distance. Caroline was talking. I knew the effort of it would make her even more tired as we got going again. For now, I would help keep her secret from the others. Her fate was not my choice. Though, it made me sad. Caroline was bright and sweet. She seemed to understand that I wasn't here to hurt anyone, least of all Jett. Soon, she'd have to make a decision unless I took it out of her hands.

I could risk it. I'd done it a hundred times for the humans who helped us in Mammoth Forest. I could take Caroline to the nearest town with a hospital. I could leave her near the entrance and slip away before anyone even knew I was there. They would care for her. She might be safe. Or it might be the very thing that brought the Pack down on the rest of them once and for all. No doubt, Caroline and the others were on a secret list somewhere like Jett said. The Pack's spies were everywhere.

Grabbing my shirt, I started to slip my arms through the sleeves. The woods around me went deathly quiet all at once. Melanie's bright laughter was the only sound. Vera said something gruff and Melanie answered her back. My wolf flared with alarm. The hair on the back of my neck stood on end.

There you are!

Able's voice filled my thoughts. My stomach rolled. My hand flew out and I dug my fingers into the rough bark of a birch tree to steady myself and feel something real. Everything in me compelled me to shout a warning to Jett. I didn't make a conscious choice to do it, but I ran. Nothing would stop me from getting to Jett's side. She was unaware. She sat at Caroline's right, her heart full of love for her.

There were two of them. I sensed them clearly. One charged in from the north, the other south. Crouching low, I skidded to a halt. Predatory instinct roared inside of me as I caught sight of the nearest wolf. His red coat made a shadowy streak as he headed for the sound of voices. His eyes gleamed as he reached the edge of the clearing. They were blood-red and trained right on Jett.

My wolf ripped out of me. No power on this earth could have kept it in check. Jett sensed me first. She was quick. Thank God, she was quick. She saw the red wolf from the corner of her eye and turned in one fluid movement, raising her rifle.

The red wolf froze, his back arched and his head low in an attack stance. His eyes glowed, fading to silver, then back to red. He was no more than five feet from Jett. Melanie's screams filled the air as Vera threw her to the ground and stood over her, rifle raised.

Twenty feet, ten, I ran as fast as I could.

Jett squeezed the trigger, hitting the red wolf straight through the heart. The sound of her gunfire drew the other wolf. He was smaller than the other but faster. His gray fur tufted off of him as he took cover under the brush. Vera sprayed the woods with her own gunfire, but she couldn't see him.

I reached the clearing. Jett was frozen to her spot, rifle raised. The red wolf had made one last, desperate charge toward her. His limbs gave out as blood poured from the gaping wound in his chest. It shouldn't have mattered. Jett's shot shouldn't have killed him that quickly. But, I knew those were no ordinary bullets. It was one more secret Jett kept to herself.

I put my body between her and the second wolf. Vera couldn't see him, but I didn't have to. She kept on shooting. In the back of my mind I realized she might be aiming for me. I didn't care. It only mattered that I got to Jett.

Getting her behind me, I turned, facing the coming threat.

You've been holding out on me, Gunnar. So this is what you've been fighting for. She's beautiful. What is her name?

No. I wouldn't. I couldn't. It was so much harder to drive out Able's voice when I was in my wolf. He wanted her name. He saw her through my eyes. Oh, God. He would make me betray her!

One thunderous shot rang out. Vera finally found her target. It took the gray wolf between the eyes. That shouldn't have been possible either. Jett and Vera were human. How in the hell had they been fast enough to hit their targets?

Baring my teeth, the danger seemed to come from all sides. There were more of them out there. There had to be.

"Go!" Jett screamed.

Vera and Melanie went for Caroline. She cried out in protest, but the two of them lifted her off the ground and started to run. Jett dug her fingers into my fur, holding me steady.

Where are you now? Hold still.

Run! I wanted to scream it. Jett wasn't safe. If she stayed by my side she wasn't safe. Able's voice wavered inside my head, untethered. When the gray wolf went down, he'd lost his grip on me. But, the pull to answer him was so strong. It sucked the air from my lungs and drove me to the ground.

"Gunnar!" Only Jett's voice reached me as I began to float away. She was on her knees in front of me, cradling my head in her hands.

"Stay with me," she said. Her eyes widened in terror. I saw myself through her. My eyes were blood-red and fading as Able Valent tried to drag me under.

Shoot me! I wanted to tell her. What if I wasn't strong enough to fight it?

"Gunnar?" Tears poured down Jett's cheeks. My heartbeat slowed even as hers jackhammered. She leaned down, putting her face within inches of mine. Her hot breath stung me; her tears fell down my snout.

Jett. Hello, Jett.

I squeezed my eyes shut. The world became the sound of my keening wail as I felt Able closing in. He could see Jett through my eyes. Oh, God. He could see her.

TWENTY-ONE

GUNNAR

"Gunnar!" Jett's palm stung my cheek and rattled my jaw as she slapped me for all she was worth. I'd shifted. I don't even remember doing it. Bile clogged my throat and I swayed on my hands and knees trying to clear my head.

I came back into myself, shuddering, panting. Jett stood before me, her rifle trained on me. Good girl, I thought. Slowly, I found the strength to stand. I put a hand up. Taking one step forward, the world spun and I doubled over again.

"Don't you dare," Jett said. She lowered her weapon and put a hand on my back. "Don't you dare go away again. Look at me."

I couldn't do it. He was close. So close. I was afraid to look at her again and give him another chance to see her.

"No!" Jett said. It was as if she were in my head as much as Able was. "Gunnar, he isn't going to win. Do you hear me? I won't let it happen. *You* won't let it happen."

"Run," I said. "Jett, get away from me. Get as far away from me as you can."

Her breath came hot, making her breasts heave. We stood inches apart. She had every reason to be afraid. I knew my wolf eyes faded in and out. I'd seen her through a red haze and knew exactly what that meant. So did she. Still, she stood her ground.

"You don't belong to him. Listen to me, dammit!" She grabbed my face in her hands, forcing me to meet her gaze. Jett's brown eyes narrowed with fierce determination. "Are you listening to me, you fucking bastard? You can't have him!"

A murderous growl filled my head, but it wasn't coming from me. It was coming from Able. But, his grip was loosening. "You're mine," Jett whispered as her tears fell again.

"Jett, no," I said. "You don't know what you're doing."

"I know exactly what I'm doing. And we should have done it a long time ago."

A beat passed. The wilderness around us went still as if it too had been waiting for this moment all along. I brought my hands up, circling them around Jett's small waist. Her eyes darted over my face. Her lips parted.

I kissed her. For years I'd been starving and I didn't even know it. When Jett leaned into the kiss and pulled me down to her, everything else fell away. She fed me her strength as her tongue darted into my mouth. I devoured her. The press of her hard nipples against my chest undid me.

Down and down we went, falling to the ground in a tangle of limbs. "Gunnar!" she gasped. Her hands were everywhere. She closed her fingers around my turgid cock and my inner wolf roared with lust.

I'd held back for so long, now the floodgates of desire opened. There was no going back. I felt Able's grip fall away like rotting vines as I gave in to my truest nature.

This. Now. I was an Alpha. Jett was my mate. We had both been born for this. Our bodies, our souls knew the way. Jett scrambled back on all fours. I took one ankle and pulled her boot off, then the other. She unfastened her pants and slid them down. I held back just enough to keep from tearing the rest of her clothes away. She yanked her top off. With it, her long, sable hair fell from the tie she'd used to keep it back, tumbling over her shoulders.

I had enough self-control to go back on my heels and look at her, truly look at her. Jett. My Jett. Every inch of her was beautiful perfection. Her heavy breasts quivered as she panted with lust. Her wine-colored nipples pebbled as the cool breeze hit them. As I crawled forward, Jett went to her back, her knees falling to the side.

A rumble of raw lust came out of me. Jett's eyes widened and her cheeks colored. I reached for her. With two fingers, I spread her soft petals and found her slick and swollen for me. Her juices flowed and she threw her head back. If she had wolf in her, she would have howled. I worked the hard little bud of her sex and she rolled her hips, beginning the ancient undulation that would bring me to her.

"Baby," I whispered, stunned I could even form words. She reached for me, closing her fingers around my cock again and drawing me close. She spread her legs wide, hooking them around my hips.

"Gunnar," she gasped. "Oh, God. You're mine!"

I was. I couldn't hold back a second longer. Jett arched her back and I plunged inside of her. I was huge and hard. Her breath caught as her walls stretched to accommodate me. I slid my hands beneath her buttocks, angling her even higher so she took me deep.

Jett slid her hands up my arms then wrapped them around my neck. I was in her all the way. Her sweet warmth enveloped me. She was home. She was safe. She was mine. Jett threw her head back and bit her lip. Her sex jumped and she thrust her hips wildly, unable to control her growing need.

I wanted more time. I wanted to draw her out, make her beg, send her to heights of pleasure she'd never known. I prayed we'd have time for it. For now, this was something different and primal.

I fucked her. Pumping my hips, I drove into her as far as she could take me. With each pounding thrust, Jett grew even wetter. She clawed my back, bringing out her own wild side. I roared with lust, my inner wolf driving me.

Yes. This. Mine.

Jett was everything. On and on I fucked her. She rose and matched me thrust for thrust, her juices coating us both. I was so full, so hard. She came suddenly, jerking around me as she sank her teeth into my shoulder, drawing blood. The pleasure and pain of it set off a chain reaction inside of me. My need thundered in my pulse and through her.

She screamed her pleasure to the trees. Every wild thing had to have heard her. It didn't matter. It was as if the world narrowed to just the two of us. As she shuddered through her climax, her limbs went slack. But I wasn't done. Oh, I was far from done.

I slid out of her. Jett's arms dropped to her sides. She caught my eyes and knew on instinct what I needed. What we both needed.

Quickly, she scrambled to her hands and knees and spread her legs wide. Oh, God. The sight of her. Gaping, wet, inviting. Light and heat seemed to pour out of me as I put a hand on her buttocks and guided her into position.

"Yes!" she cried as I entered her again. Deeper this time. Oh, so deep.

Jett's hair fell to the side, exposing the nape of her neck. As I arched my back and drove into her, my feral nature took over.

"Gunnar, please!" she begged. There was no going back. Not now. Not ever. The time for reason had passed. She seemed to understand I couldn't stop unless she asked me too. She didn't. Instead, Jett reached back and gathered her hair in one hand. She arched her back and presented her neck to me.

"Please," she gasped one last time.

As my seed poured into her, I leaned far forward. Jett dropped her hair and gripped the ground, bracing herself. My fangs dropped just enough and I sank them into the soft spot at the nape of her neck.

The world opened up. Colors became brighter. Electricity sparked between us, kindling my nerve endings. I felt Jett's do the same. I felt everything about her as I made my mark and bound her to me forever.

TWENTY-TWO

JETT

Gunnar was everything. He spread me open and filled me with heat, light, energy. As his teeth sank into the soft flesh at the nape of my neck, a burst of pain blazed a path down my spine. Just as quickly, it gave way to the deepest pleasure I'd ever known.

I saw myself through Gunnar's eyes. He'd made me a wanton, wild thing. Oh, it felt so good. Colors became more vibrant. My sense of smell, keener. Even the earth beneath my fingertips felt different. Then there was Gunnar himself. Before, I'd felt his pulse along with my own. Now, there was no distinguishing them. We were one. His heart beat for mine and mine for him.

My Alpha. My mate.

A fresh orgasm ripped through me. It was quicker than the first, but even more intense. I sensed he could bring me to it over and over if we had the time. Oh, what I wouldn't give for more time.

Gunnar emptied himself in me. At the same time, I felt myself filling him too. True mates. Fated. How could I have waited so long for this? We both tumbled to the ground, exhausted. Gunnar slid his arms around me, cradling my body with his. I felt safe, warm, protected. If only we could have stayed like this forever.

But, we were not that lucky. We both knew it. Able was gone. Gunnar didn't have to tell me. I could *feel* his thoughts even if I couldn't hear them. He was grounded now, centered. He was with me.

"Are you okay?" he finally said, his eyes shining silver. I felt his need to shift ripple through me. It was like a second hunger. He kept it at bay.

I sat up, feeling suddenly shy. He reached for me, gently grasping my nipple. A moan of pleasure escaped from me, unbidden. Oh, I wanted him again already.

"I'm okay," I said. Reality started to close around us. What we'd shared had shifted my world on its axis. And yet, the danger hadn't passed.

Gunnar sensed my mood. He sat up and we scrambled for our clothes. "We have to find the others," he said.

"The Pack?" I asked, my voice cracking.

"No," he said. "Listen. It's quiet now."

I closed my eyes and did as he bid me. At first, I heard the normal sounds of nature. The leaves skittered in the wind; a mourning dove warbled in the distance. Then, slowly, it was as if a second layer of hearing opened up for me. Everything became sharper. It was Gunnar. When he marked me, somehow I could hear *through* him.

My hand went to the mark he'd made at the base of my neck. Already, it had begun to heal. I wished I could see it. On instinct, I knew it was nothing like the one Melanie had. Hers stayed angry. Mine was faint, almost as if it had always been there. It was a part of me. It wasn't something that had been *done* to me.

Gunnar was already up and dressed. My limbs felt heavy as I pulled my shirt over my head. Our mating had been a serious workout. Heat flared between my legs at just the thought of it. Oh, I wanted so much more.

He went to the two dead wolves, checking for signs of life. I knew he'd find none. I hit the red one straight through the heart. Vera's shot had hit the other in his frontal lobe. No shifter I knew could survive a direct hit with our poison-laced bullets. And that was the last secret I'd kept from Gunnar.

"How?" he asked, turning to me. My old defenses fell away. I was more a part of Gunnar than the Twelve. I knew that with each new beat of my heart. His heart.

"Those weren't regular bullets. They're laced with a neurotoxin that's deadly to shifters if we hit the target."

"Brain and heart," he answered. He reached down and felt inside the red wolf's wound. With a grisly pop, Gunnar pulled the bullet out. It was flat and misshapen, but even now my heart flared with alarm. I had no idea if the toxin would affect Gunnar just by touching it.

He held it up, examining it. Then, he slid it into his back pocket. He went to the gray wolf and retrieved the other bullet. "There's no point letting the Pack get their hands on it. They took Lowell, but let's not give them any more help."

"We should get moving," I said, slinging my rifle back over my shoulder. "Vera and the others can't have gone far. You sure those were the only two?"

Gunnar nodded. "Yeah. Able's gone too. Without them and without...me...I think he's blind where we're concerned. We just bought some time. That's all. You know he's going to come back harder next time. As far as he's concerned, we can't win."

I swallowed hard and went to him. "I know," I said. I saw doubt and fear cloud his eyes. I wouldn't let it. "Gunnar, I know. And I wouldn't change a damn thing. I will *not* lose you to him. Do you hear me?"

He cupped my jaw in his palm, running his thumb along my cheekbone. "I won't lose you either. I'm going to figure out a way to get you over the border where you'll be safe."

I noted that he didn't say "we." My heart dropped, but there was no time to argue. Vera and Melanie wouldn't make it far trying to carry Caroline. Whether Vera liked it or not, she needed Gunnar and she needed me.

"Can you sense which direction they went?" I asked. Gunnar lifted his chin and sniffed the wind.

"Due north," he finally said. "They've taken to the water. Smart."

He held a hand out to me. Smiling, I took it. There was one more secret he hadn't asked me to tell. Magic bullets were one thing. Getting a shot off quicker than a shifter could move was something else.

————

Something was happening to me. With each step we took, my connection to Gunnar solidified. I couldn't sense what he sensed, but I understood every move he made. We traveled along the water's edge. The pungent scent of brine and seaweed would better mask our own. He kept tilting his head toward the southwest, pausing for no more than a second or two. Each time, my breath caught waiting for some telltale sign from Gunnar that he sensed something. But, his heartbeat stayed steady and so did mine.

My growing need for him didn't change. It gripped me like a second hunger, but the timing couldn't be worse. Vera and the others had too much of a head start. Alone, Gunnar could have caught up to them in no more than an hour. I slowed him down. He never said anything, but it was obvious. I had just two human legs to travel with.

"Come here," he said after we'd crossed the narrowest part of the rushing stream. Gunnar hadn't yet asked me where we were going. Sure, he could easily pick up Caroline, Melanie, or Vera's scent but he let me lead the way. Reaching for me, he hoisted me up to a rock ledge overlooking the Golden Rock Dam. The water slammed into the rocks below us. It was a twenty-foot drop. Far enough to kill me if I lost my footing. Gunnar held me steady.

I lost my balance and crashed into him chest to chest. Laughing, my arms went up, gripping his strong shoulders. Gunnar's smile melted the growing chill I felt as the sun began to set. Leaning down, he kissed me.

"You sure you're okay?" he asked. Heat rushed through me. Oh, I wanted him again, badly. We'd stopped once since he'd marked me in the big woods for a quick coupling. It helped clear my head. I'd need it again soon.

"I have no idea," I answered. "This is new for me."

"It's new for me too," he smiled. "And it's the lousiest timing ever. Jett, do you realize what could happen if the Pack ever gets close enough?"

"They won't," I said. "I told you. Where we're going? It's safe. And in case you haven't noticed, I'm not defenseless."

"I did notice that. That's a different conversation we're going to need to have. Soon."

A flare of alarm went through me, an old instinct. I'd viewed men like Gunnar as the enemy for so long, it was hard to switch my mental gears sometimes.

"It's just up ahead," I said, pointing beyond the ridge. Our summer encampment allowed us to hide in plain sight.

Gunnar jutted his chin and letting his gaze follow my finger. "I know," he said. "Vera's hiding on the other side of the bluff. She's upwind thinking I can't scent her."

Alarm fluttered through me. "Gunnar, let me go on ahead. All she's going to need to do is take one look at us to know..."

"To know what?" he said, running a hand down my arm. The last rays of sunlight danced in Gunnar's blue eyes. "That I'd die before I let anything happen to you? That somebody's going to have to get help for Caroline, and soon? I'm stronger. I move faster. If I can get to them, I know people who can help. It might not be too late to save her without bringing the whole Pack down on our heads."

"How exactly do you plan on doing that?" Vera came out from

behind a thick oak tree, training her rifle straight at Gunnar. Gunnar didn't so much as flinch or turn his back. Of course he knew she'd been standing there the entire time.

I couldn't be mad at her. Instead, my heart flooded with relief. She was safe. That meant Melanie was too. Since we hadn't found Caroline abandoned on the side of the trail, that could only mean they'd managed to get her into the hideout safely too.

Smiling, Gunnar put a possessive hand on my back and turned to her. "The same way I've been surviving all along. I'm fast. I'm quiet. And I know who I can trust."

Vera snorted. She still hadn't lowered her weapon. I made a move to try and put myself in front of Gunnar. He held me back.

"She won't hurt me," I said, trying to push forward. Again, Gunnar stopped me. He emitted a low growl I knew only I could hear. It did something to me, making every muscle in my body go rigid. It wasn't permanent, but it was a clear, preternatural command for me to stay still. I recognized it instantly for what it was: my Alpha trying to protect me. Only, I was more worried about Vera trying to hurt him.

"Vera," Gunnar said through tight lips. I felt his pulse race with barely contained anger. "What else do I need to do to prove to you that I'm on your side?"

It sounded good when I said it. Vera didn't drop her weapon, but she dropped her right shoulder slightly, as if letting some of the tension out of it. She was just as tired as the rest of us.

"Gunnar will sleep outside," I said. "Like always." What I didn't say was that I'd stay right by his side. Vera gave no indication that she realized what had happened between Gunnar and me.

I would tell her tonight, after everyone had a full belly and a clearer mind.

"You need me," Gunnar said. "You might be able to fend off one or two members of the Pack at a time, but not if you don't know when they're coming. I do. Jett...go with her and make sure--"

Gunnar's voice was cut off by Melanie's scream. In the same instant, Gunnar's wolf eyes flashed silver. Vera whirled around and raised her rifle. I moved toward the sound and Gunnar grabbed my arm, holding me back.

"Vera! I can't wake her up!" Melanie's anguished cry cut through me. Vera was already on the move. She'd given up aiming her weapon and slung it over her shoulder as she broke into a run. Gunnar and I followed close behind.

We ran down the steep embankment leading to our hideout below the dam. Years ago, during construction, they'd built diversion tunnels. Abandoned now, they'd never been filled in. We had a protected position at the base of a viaduct crossing the Rockcastle River. Melanie was there, leaning against the high cement wall, cradling Caroline in her lap.

Caroline's color had gone gray. Her eyes were open and unfocused. Gunnar got to her first, skidding to a halt in front of Melanie. He dropped to his knees and put a hand to Caroline's forehead.

"She's breathing," he said. "But it's labored and shallow. Jett, she's burning up."

Vera tossed her rifle to the ground and went to Melanie's side. Caroline's mouth hung slack. Her lips were dry and cracked.

"I was afraid of this," Gunnar said. "She was worse off than she wanted to let on. The infection is deep. She knew I could scent it."

"Why didn't you say something?" Vera said, her tone thick with accusation.

"Say what?" Gunnar shot back. "Exactly what would you have done if I had? I'll tell you. You would have told me to mind my own business and remind me how long you've been looking after everybody before I came along."

Vera's mouth hung open, but at Gunnar's tirade, she snapped it shut. She knew he was right. And my heart dropped with the sickening clarity that none of it mattered one damn bit anymore. Caroline was dying.

"It's probably a coma," Gunnar said. "Shit. I can't help her from here. We have to get her to someone who can if it's not already too late."

"It's not safe," Melanie pleaded. "They're out there. I can still *feel* him." Tears streamed down her face. For a moment, Vera tried to shush her and calm her with a hand against her cheek. It took almost a full minute before Melanie's truth washed over her.

"What do you mean you can feel *him*?" she asked. Melanie didn't look at her. Instead, she locked eyes with Gunnar. For the first time, I fully understood what Melanie meant. Gunnar was *in* me since he'd marked me. Though we hadn't tested it out, I knew with absolute certainty, if we were separated, he would be able to call to me. He had claimed me as my Alpha. Dear God, in Melanie's case it had happened by force.

"Where's the nearest town?" Gunnar asked, turning to me.

"Clarksville," I said. "About seven miles due east. There's not much there. A hospital, I think. I don't know how good it is."

"She needs intensive care," Gunnar said. "If I can get her there alive, maybe they can either help her or get her transferred to Lexington or someplace better. It's the only shot she's got."

He'd already made up his mind. Scooping Caroline out of Melanie's lap as if she weighed nothing, he stood. Caroline's head lolled to the side. If Gunnar hadn't checked, I would have thought she was dead already. Her sightless eyes rolled in the back of her head.

"Gunnar," I said, my voice dropping low. My throat clogged with growing panic as I realized what he meant to do. He meant to leave.

"I'll be back," he said.

"If you get caught..." Vera said.

Gunnar turned to her. "If I get caught, Jett will know."

No. I couldn't stand it. The idea of being separated from Gunnar right now sent my heart racing. Panic washed over me, making me shiver.

"Let me go with you," I said. "I know this area better than you do." It was a futile argument. Gunnar didn't need a tour guide. He could probably find his way to the closest town with his eyes closed just by following his nose. He could cover more ground faster than any of us and he could carry Caroline with no effort at all.

"Listen to me," he said. Gunnar came to me. He leaned forward, pressing his forehead against mine as he held Caroline's limp form between us. I put a hand to her cheek. Her skin blazed with fever. "Stay out of sight. No matter what happens. No matter what you think you feel."

"Gunnar, you have to come back," I said.

"I will. I always will."

He kissed me quickly, leaving me breathless. A look passed between him and Vera, then he turned toward the setting sun and bounded up the embankment.

TWENTY-THREE

GUNNAR

She would die. Caroline had never been anything but sweet to me. She, like the others, had every reason *not* to trust me, and yet she had. Today, it was with her life. With each step I took, my wolf raged to get out.

This was a waste. All of it. Caroline couldn't be more than twenty-five or twenty-six years old. But, as I held her limp body in my arms, she looked frail and old. She'd lost so much weight and water, her skin was almost translucent. A web of dark veins popped at her temples. She wore jeans and a loose-fitting red t-shirt. Her right leg swelled and went stiff, her body riddled with infection. I should have followed my instincts days ago. Screw Vera, I should have brought Caroline to safety.

Clarksville was easy to find. A small, rural town, it sat nestled in a deep in the river valley. As I emerged from the woods, I sank low, hiding us both among the foliage. From here, I could see the whole town spread out in a grid. Dawn was just about to break.

Clarksville had a single church in the northeast quadrant of town. The safest thing might be to take Caroline there. Safest for me, but possibly deadly for her. No. I would have to bring her straight to the emergency room of whatever hospital I could find.

I scanned the town then closed my eyes, letting my keener senses lead the way. There. Almost dead center. At five stories, it was the tallest building in town. I would have to move faster than any non-shifters could see. There was no way to escape notice if I waltzed through the streets carrying Caroline's limp form in my arms.

She murmured something past dry lips, her agony written in the deep lines above her brow. "Shhh," I whispered. "It's going to be all right. I'll make sure of it."

She didn't deserve this. She should be graduating from college or getting married or doing whatever it was that normal twenty-somethings do. Instead, she'd spent years living in fear and hiding from the ruthless, vindictive Pack patrols, afraid for her life.

"It's all right, Caro," I said. "I've got you."

The truth was, I had no idea if she was going to be all right. The infection had spread so fast, it might be too late to save her. Rage tore through me. It wasn't fair. Because, no matter what, I couldn't stay with her. I could only get her to people with the expertise to help her if they could. But, she would wake up alone and afraid. I couldn't even risk leaving a note or word with what happened to the rest of her friends.

The hair prickled at the back of my neck. A heavy band pressed around my head. The Pack wasn't far. I couldn't sense them in town, but there was movement to the northeast. We were so close to the Tennessee border here. I'd downplayed it to Jett. I told her we'd never seen Pack this far. I think even she knew the opposite was true, but she didn't question me. We all knew it was either this or we'd all sealed Caroline's fate.

I gathered her close to me and started to run. My wolf clamored to get out as the scent of the Pack drew closer. They wouldn't be looking for me here. Hell, they'd never think I was dumb enough to come waltzing into a populated area like this. If I was quick enough, I'd get in and out before any of them were the wiser.

The irony was, the thing that made me safer was also the thing that could put Jett in harm's way. Marking her had strengthened my inner Alpha to the point I couldn't hear Able Valent at all anymore. Maybe that would change if I ever came face to face with him again. For now, he couldn't touch me. But, if he got close to Jett...

I pushed it out of my mind. Two orderlies leaned against the wall near a dumpster in the alley. The blazing red lights of the emergency room were just ahead. The smoke from their cigarettes reached me. I moved by them in a blur.

The ER opened into a large waiting room. Glass separated it from the main hospital. I had to get past a receptionist at a long, U-shaped counter. She didn't look up from her computer screen as I approached. A few of the other patients did. Jaws dropped at the sight of me. It wasn't even Caroline's lifeless form that caught their attention. It was me. This was Kentucky. They knew what I was.

I saw an empty wheelchair against the wall and carefully put Caroline into it. Her head lolled to the side, but she didn't fall. I wheeled her up to the counter and cleared my throat. Finally, the receptionist looked up; her owl-like eyes widened even further.

"Can I help you?" she asked.

"No," I said. "But you have to help her."

She looked at Caroline and quickly got to her feet. She pressed a button on the side of her workstation. She was either calling for security or medical help. Either way, I knew I couldn't stick around to find out. Though it killed me to do it, I had to run. Somewhere, deep inside this building, I felt the Pack. Able had maybe one or two members here. They didn't sense me yet, but they would.

I leaned down and pressed my mouth against Caroline's ear. I didn't know if she could hear me. Probably not. But I had to at least try.

"Stay strong," I said. "Stay alive. I'll try to figure out a way to get word to you. Smart people who care about you won't forget you."

Then, I turned and let my wolf out just enough to give me the speed I needed. Those still waiting in chairs would only feel a strong breeze and see a shadow. By the time the Pack felt anything, I had hoped to be long gone.

I said a silent prayer for Caroline and headed back for the woods where I belonged. Jett's heartbeat thundered inside of me like a beacon calling me home. She was scared. It would only be about four hours from the time I left her side to when I returned. Even that was too long.

I *needed* Jett. Jagger and Liam had tried to tell me what it was like to have a fated mate. It seemed starry-eyed and foolish. Also careless and dangerous. The thing Jagger feared over all else had happened. The Pack had used his mate Keara against him...or tried to. She died before they could torture our location out of her. Losing her had split Jagger's mind apart. He might never be the same.

And now, I understood that he would likely do it all over again for just one more day with her. Jett was part of me. I would live and bleed for her for the rest of my days. Even the thought of any danger coming to her stirred my wolf to rage. Every inch separating us cut into me like a thousand daggers. It was like trying to breathe underwater.

One thing was certain: once I got back to her, I wouldn't leave her side again. Golden Rock wasn't safe. It was a good hideout since they had access to clean water and shelter. It was so far away from the nearest town that the Pack likely didn't patrol there often. The viaduct provided a perfect place for a sentry so Vera or Jett could have easily kept watch before I came along. But, now that I *had* come along, they were too open. I couldn't stay above ground for long periods of time anymore. And, I'd be damned if I'd leave Jett behind.

As day bled into evening again, I heard the rushing waters of the river and Jett's steady heartbeat beneath it. She would probably sense my question before I asked it, but there was only one place safe enough for Jett to be.

It was time to go back to Mammoth Forest.

TWENTY-FOUR

GUNNAR

I saw Jett's silhouette as I approached. She stood sentry at the top of the viaduct. Her shoulders went stiff. She sensed me. Slowly, she turned around and lowered her rifle. I knew she could see my wolf eyes glinting in the darkness. I ran to her so fast it had to look like flying to her.

"Gunnar!" she shouted. She dropped her rifle and ran into my arms. It had been less than a day since we parted. It was way too long.

Her hair was soft and clean; her scent washed over me, stirring my lust. "Baby," I whispered, my lips finding hers. She was pliant, breathless. Her hard nipples brushed against my chest. She smoothed her hands over my face, down my shoulders, then circled them around my waist.

"You're okay? They didn't follow you?"

"No," I said. "I got Caroline to the hospital in Clarksville. It killed me to leave her. I just pray to God we got her to help in time."

Tears streamed down Jett's cheeks. "She's going to be so afraid. If she wakes up...when she wakes up. She's going to think we abandoned her."

"She won't," I said. "She'll know that her friends did everything they could to keep her safe. And she'll know that she's alive because of you. What about you? Any sign of the Pack out here?"

I knew the answer was no. Connected as I was to Jett, I would have felt any alarm she did. As I held her in my arms, a different growing need rose. Jett's lips parted and she kissed me. I felt the slow heat build between her legs even from here.

"God, Gunnar," she gasped. "Why can't I get enough of you?"

I chuckled softly as I pressed my lips against her forehead. "I'm sorry, baby. I probably should have warned you about the Rise."

"The Rise?" She pulled back and eyed me with suspicion.

"I'm new at this too," I said. "Before I met you, I was convinced I'd be a bachelor wolf my whole life. Mates seemed to be nothing but trouble."

"Oh, really?" she swatted my ass. "You better talk, Cole."

"Uh...well...uh...there are probably a billion other people better than explaining this than me, but the Rise is what happens after you take a mate. The first marking isn't enough. You need more. Many, many more." I couldn't help the sultry growl that escaped from me.

Jett shuddered in my arms. Her nipples got even harder. I

couldn't help myself. I slid my fingers under her shirt and found her breasts. She groaned and her knees turned to rubber.

"Come on," I said. "I need you. I don't mean to wait."

"I...have...to...keep...watch," Jett spoke through kisses.

"Baby, you don't think I'm going to sense the Pack miles away? It's quiet. I promise. We have time. A few minutes at least. It's for your own good. You'll get sick if we don't..."

"Mmm." Whatever protest Jett wanted to make, it died on her lips as I lifted her off the ground. She wrapped her legs around me. I carried her to the end of the viaduct. Melanie and Vera had taken refuge deeper in the woods.

I took Jett to a clearing in the shadow of the bridge. For a moment, it felt like we were the only two people in the world. Later, we might be blessed with more time. I would tease her out, torture her with my tongue, bring her to the edge of pleasure and back again while she cried out for me. Now, the driving need we both felt controlled us.

I placed her gently on the ground. Jett scrambled back and wriggled out of her pants. She set her rifle to the side, close enough that she could reach it quickly if danger came. She spread her legs wide for me as she leaned back on her elbows. I reached for her, pushing her t-shirt up and her bra with it. Her tits popped out and my vision tunneled. I knew my eyes went pure silver as lust coursed through me.

I lunged for her, grasping her nipple gently between my teeth. Jett arched her back and cried out. She threaded her fingers through my hair and pulled me down to her. My Jett wanted it rough tonight. Sucking one nipple, I rolled it with my tongue, loving the way it pebbled. I reached between her legs. She was dripping wet already. I kneaded her taut little sex between my fingers. She gasped and spread her legs even wider.

I got my own jeans off and tore my shirt over my head before going to work on her other nipple. Jett started to thrust her hips wildly. I think I could have made her come just by working her nipples, she was so ready for me. I slid three fingers inside of her, loving the way her juices coated my hand and her walls clenched. She was my sustenance, my everything. I came to life when she found me.

"Gunnar!" she gasped, reaching the peak of pleasure. Not yet, I thought. Not yet. I slid my fingers out of her as she stroked my cock. She would feel so good, so warm.

Jett moved. Her eyes snapped open, dark with lust. She pushed up until she knelt before me. I threw my head back and roared with desire as she fastened her lips around me. With her eyes locked on mine, she sucked me, taking me deep into her throat. My knees trembled as I tried to hold on.

Lacing my fingers through her hair, I spurred her on. I fucked Jett's mouth as the tide of pleasure rose in me. I'd intended to tease her, draw her out. She turned the tables on me. She owned me with her mouth and I held on for the ride.

"Baby," I whispered. "What you do to me."

Jett redoubled her efforts, taking me so deeply. She went on her hands and knees, stroking me with her tongue, her lips, grazing me gently with her teeth. She claimed me in her own way, just as I had done her. I doubled over, running a hand along her spine.

Her movements were slow, rhythmic and sultry at first. As she sucked harder, they became more wild, reckless. Her own need built. I threw my head back, unable to hold on a second longer. Jett reached for me, driving my cock deep into her mouth as she gently stroked my balls. It was all I could take. I let go, pouring myself into her. She took me in, drop for precious drop.

I felt like I could come in her forever. When the tide receded, she licked me clean and leaned back, releasing me with a pop. Just a thin membrane separated me from my wolf. Oh, he wanted out.

Jett already knew what to do. She turned, offering me her backside. She dug her fingers into the soft earth, bracing herself. Her hair fell to the side. The silvery crescent-shaped mark I'd made at the base of her neck stood out against her smooth, supple skin.

I plunged into her, sheathing myself to the root. Jett cried out with pleasure. She thrust backward, dropping her chin almost to the ground. I placed one hand on her hip to steady her, then leaned far forward, my fangs already out.

As Jett came around me, rocketing back and forth, I marked her a second time. She tasted so good. She jerked and bucked, taking me in. I licked her tiny wound. It would close even before her pleasure waned. This deeper mark would bind her to me even more and might lessen her need just a little. At least, she'd be able to go longer without the urge to mate overpowering her. The wicked part of me wanted to keep her on edge. God how I loved watching her squirm with lust for me.

Slowly, gracefully, Jett fell to her side as I withdrew. She smiled up at me, spent. I went to her, curving my body around hers.

"That was..." she said, breathless. "I don't even..."

"Amazing?" I said, nipping her ear.

"I just don't know why I ever thought I should hold you off."

I couldn't help but laugh. I reached for her, tweaking her swollen nipple.

"Mmm," she said. "Don't tease. I feel like every nerve ending in my body is on fire right now."

I kissed the back of her neck, loving the contour of the mark she now bore. "Come on," I said. "Back to work." I gave her a playful swat on her ass.

Jett squealed with delight. We fumbled for our clothes and got dressed.

"Why don't you go get some sleep?" I said. "I'm too keyed up. I'll stand watch."

I reached for her, offering my hand. Jett took it and rose on shaky legs. Oh, I liked that too. "We'll watch together," she said. "You think I can sleep after that?"

She went up on her tiptoes and kissed me. I curved my arm around her waist, pulling her to me. Then, we walked back up the hill and took a position at the top of the bridge.

———

Jett's stomach growled something fierce as the sun rose over the hill.

Vera emerged from the woods first, followed by Melanie. They approached us holding hands, their expressions stern. A pit formed in my stomach. I wished I had better news to give them about Caroline.

Vera slid her arm around Melanie's waist. The two of them

looked like they hadn't slept a wink. Guilt washed over me. I should have gone to them earlier to tell them what I knew.

"She's settled then?" Vera asked. The last twenty-four hours had thawed something between us. Vera knew the risk I'd taken to help Caroline. I could have kept on going. I knew a part of her probably hoped I had.

"Yes," I answered. I gave her the highlights of what had happened in Clarksville. I knew it wasn't satisfying. I'd love to have been able to tell her I'd stayed by Caroline's side and watched her get better right before my eyes. But, none of us believed in fairytales. The odds of Caroline surviving were slim.

"Thank you," Melanie said. She let go of Vera's hand and came to me. She touched my cheek, her eyes glistening. "I know what that could have cost you."

I gave her a solemn nod. "You've risked plenty for me. All of you. If it's within my power, I'll send help for her."

Vera's chin dropped. It was an odd gesture for her. I was used to her standing so tall and defiant. A look passed between her and Melanie. Something had been decided. I knew on instinct I wasn't going to like it.

"Jett," Vera said. "I think it's time for us to face some hard truths."

"Don't start," Jett said. She kept a vice-like grip on my hand. "Gunnar has proved over and over he's an asset to us. He stays. Period. You know if we put it to a vote Caroline would agree."

"I knew you'd say that," Vera said. To her credit, she at least had the decency to look miserable. "And I'm not asking Gunnar to leave. I am. I mean...we are. Melanie and me."

"What are you saying?" Jett's skin flashed cold where I held her. Her pulse quickened. I pulled her to me.

"Jett, I'm sorry," Melanie said. "You knew this was coming. Gunnar, I like you. I know you aren't like the others. It took me a long time to see that, but I do. It's only...that just doesn't change the fact that the longer you're around, the easier it's going to be for the Pack to find us. I also know I can't ask Jett to leave you. So, it's time for us to go our separate ways."

"No!" Jett's anguished cry jolted me. My wolf flared and I pulled her to me, wanting to protect her from even emotional pain. I knew I couldn't.

"Jett," I said. She would hate me for what I had to say, but Vera and Melanie were right. Just not for the reasons they thought.

"It's not safe enough for any of you here," I said. "Your cave and the tunnels were better. At least you could get underground. You know that's the safest. Especially for you, Mel. The Pack has a much harder time sensing you or me there. Even that's not perfect though."

"What are you suggesting?" Jett turned to me.

I took a hard breath. I had wanted to broach this with her alone. "It's time for me to take you back to the closest thing I have to home. It's better for all of us if I don't tell you where that is. And I won't lie. We're going to have to cut through some of the most dangerous territories in Kentucky to get there. But, it's the one place I know I can keep you safe."

"Me?" Jett said. She let go of my hand and took a step back. "You mean us. All of us."

My stare locked on Vera's. She knew. She'd always known. She kept a strong hand on Melanie's shoulder as tears fell down her face.

"I can't go with you," Melanie said, her voice breaking. "As long as the monster who marked me is still alive, I'm a threat to you. I can't know where Gunnar's resistance fighters live. He could follow me too easily there."

"Then we don't go," Jett said, stomping her foot. "None of us. We stay here."

Vera let go of Melanie and put her hands on Jett's shoulders, turning her to face her. "No. We don't. I love you like my sister. But, you made your choice with Gunnar. I don't blame you. If he is to you even half of what Melanie is to me, it was no choice at all. So go. Be safe. And I'm not taking no for an answer."

Vera pulled Jett to her. Jett's face went white and her jaw dropped as Vera hugged her close. She squeezed her eyes shut and cried.

TWENTY-FIVE

JETT

O nce the decision was made, there was nothing more to say. My heart broke into a million pieces even as my bond with Gunnar grew. Rather than leaving right away, we thought it best to wait a few days just to make sure the Pack hadn't picked up Gunnar's trail when he left Clarksville. I wanted desperately to head back down there to see if we could get news about Caroline.

Vera and Melanie would leave first. Gunnar had finally convinced them that Golden Rock wasn't safe in the long term. If they couldn't find a way to cross over the Tennessee border, they needed someplace where they could get underground quickly. Vera agreed, but said little. I knew her too well. There was one more place we knew to go. We'd found one more tunnel system along the Cumberland River. Backtracking had its downsides, but with just the two of them traveling together, I felt sure they could make it.

In the middle of our last night as a group, Gunnar told me the secret he'd been keeping since the day I met him. I held my breath as he spoke, knowing he'd been tortured for this very information. Telling me now would be his penultimate act of trust. Taking me there was all that was left.

He scratched a map into the dirt with his fingers. "Shadow Springs is here," he said. "The Mammoth Cave system, the one the public knows about, stretches through here. Patrols are weak here. Or at least, they were as of a year ago. Able had one of his generals stationed here with a cadre of patrols. We took them out."

"You killed them? All of them?"

"Most of them," he answered. "Before that, we couldn't spend much time topside without the Pack sensing us. Now...or at least, before I left for Birch Haven, we'd weakened the Alpha's hold enough so we could."

"You think it's still that safe now?" I hugged my knees to my chest. Shadow Springs would take us days to get to if we went on foot. Gunnar had a plan to steal a car. I wasn't sure how I felt about that. Any attention from law enforcement meant potential Pack attention. They knew what to monitor and the Pack had infiltrated every branch of government in the state. Underground and off the grid was the safest bet for everyone.

"I think it's worth the risk," he said. "Plus, why would Able have tried so hard to get that intel from me if he already had it? No. We're not Pack...but it's just a feeling I have. My friends are still there. Mammoth Forest is still the base of operations."

I rested my chin on my knees. Gunnar tapped the ground with his stick, deep in concentration. He had a plan B, I knew. But, he wouldn't tell me what it was. He'd marked me two more times in the last couple of days. Soon, I knew I'd be able to read some of his thoughts and him mine. I welcomed that, but at the same time it scared me.

For now, we read each other's moods and Gunnar was worried. I reached for him, running a hand over his bare shoulder. His muscles rippled at my touch. He regarded me with those keen, silver wolf eyes that always flared when he was aroused. An answering heat blossomed between my legs. There would be time enough for that soon. For now, I knew he had questions.

"Someday soon," he said. "You're going to have to tell me how you were quick enough to shoot that wolf the other day."

"I know," I said. My answer surprised him. I would have told him then and there, but Gunnar put up a hand to stop me.

"When we get to Mammoth Forest," he said. "When I know for sure I can keep you safe."

His eyes clouded with worry. Though I couldn't yet read his mind, I knew what troubled him. Marking me let him sense my well-being. It was meant so he could protect me. But it would also make it easier for the Pack to use me against him if they ever captured one of us. He said he could feel my pain. I believed him. Leaning forward, I kissed him.

He held my chin with his fingers. "You know if I could safely bring Vera and Melanie to Mammoth Forest, I would. I'd kill for either of them if it came to it."

"I know," I said, my throat growing thick with emotion. "The same reason you don't want me to tell you about how I killed that beta. That's why you're afraid of Melanie knowing about Mammoth Forest."

His Adam's apple bobbed as he swallowed hard. "Yes. As long as the wolf who marked her lives, he'll be able to track her."

"Gunnar," I said. "I've been thinking about that. A lot. I know you're probably not going to like this, but it's why I think that when we leave...we should leave all of the weapons with Vera. She'll need every advantage she can get against the Pack."

"No!" he said. "You've proven to me more than once that you can handle yourself against at least the patrols if it's one on one. I will not leave you defenseless."

"I'm not defenseless. I have you."

"No," he said, his voice dropping. "You'll take the nine at least. Let Vera and Melanie have the rifles. How much of your special ammo do you have left?"

He wasn't going to like my answer. I gave it with a sigh. "One magazine for the nine. Plus one in the chamber. Vera's got enough ammo of her own to last a little while. But, when it's gone. It's gone."

He scratched his chin. "There's got to be a way to get more."

I shrugged. "We've tried. I told you. We had help at the beginning from some of the shifters at Birch Haven. They gave us what they could but never told us where it came from. They're all dead now as far as I know."

"Maybe Liam and the others will have an idea about it. Our contacts through the state run deep. Somebody's had to have heard at least rumors here and there. We ran into some northern shifters a few years back. I watched them kill a Pack wolf with a gunshot. I thought it was just a lucky one, but maybe it was more than that. It's a long shot, but it's hope."

"Liam," I said. "And there's Mac and Payne. Your other friend is Jagger?"

Gunnar's expression darkened, but he nodded. Five Alphas. A tremor went through me. I was just beginning to truly understand how powerful Gunnar was as opposed to the beta Pack members we'd encountered so far. I couldn't imagine what being in a room with five at once was like. Would they like me? Would they be angry that Gunnar chose a mate without discussing it with them first?

Gunnar's soft laughter sent a thrill of excitement through me. He kissed my hand, his eyes sparkling with mischief. "They're going to love you. And I can't wait for you to meet Molly. She's Liam's mate. Since Keara died, she tries to be the boss of us. You remind me of her a lot. And if Mac got out with Eve..."

His voice trailed off. He'd told me Eve was the girl his friend Mac found at Birch Haven along with his sister. If they were back in Mammoth Forest, they might know more about Jade's sister Jasmine. My heart fluttered with hope. Gunnar didn't say it, but I knew there might even be a chance that Jasmine was *in* Mammoth Forest. He had no idea where the women went after he and his friends liberated the college.

"Come on," he said. "We have a big day tomorrow and a long way to travel. You need to get some sleep."

"What about you?" I settled against him.

"I don't need as much sleep as you do. Let me take watch tonight. You, Vera and Melanie could use a break."

Earlier, Vera had chosen a rare moment to agree with Gunnar on that score. Ever since he came back from Clarksville, they'd reached a detente. It didn't mean she trusted him, but she finally believed he wasn't actively or inadvertently trying to bring the Pack down on our heads. Plus, her mind was full of worry for Melanie. For now, there was nothing I could do but pray.

———

Though Gunnar kept watch, I didn't get much sleep that night. We all woke at dawn. Melanie had already packed everything. Either she'd discussed it with Gunnar or come to the same conclusion herself, but she handed me the nine as we headed up the embankment alongside the viaduct together. Melanie had a rifle strapped to her back. Vera carried the rest of their supplies. Over Mel's protests, we'd given them all the food. Gunnar was adamant that he could hunt for the two of us with half the effort. Plus, if his car theft plan worked, we'd be in Mammoth Forest in less than twenty-four hours. The thought sent a shiver of excitement and terror through me. He sensed it and took my hand.

"Be careful," I said to Vera, my throat clogged with emotion. "Don't do anything I wouldn't do out there. I'm going to find a way to get word to you."

"Don't worry," she said, hugging me. "I can take care of myself. Hell, I've been taking care of *your* ass for years. You're still whole last time I checked."

"Shit," I said laughing. "You like to talk a big talk, Vee. You'd be nowhere if it weren't for me."

I meant it as a joke, just as she had, but my words settled heavily over both of us. Vera and I had had each other's backs for so long, I didn't know how it would feel not knowing where she was every second of the day. She'd been my rock. We'd buried so many friends together. Hot tears stung my eyes, but I refused to shed them. So did she.

"Don't say the 'g' word," she said. "Just say I'll see you around. Because I will. That's a promise."

Smiling, I broke away from her first. Vera wasn't one to make promises. Her words meant everything. Gunnar stood behind me, looming large and solid. God, how I wanted to tell Vera where we were going. I felt torn between the people who'd helped me make it this far and the strangers I'd rely on from now on. In the center of all of that was Gunnar. I'd only known him for a few weeks, and yet, I knew I belonged by his side. Vera knew it too. She couldn't bring herself to tell him that, but in a way her silence said it all.

Gunnar reached forward and shook her hand. Then, he went to Melanie, hugging her close. "I'm so sorry," he told her softly. "If a day comes when I can find your wolf and kill him, know that I will."

"I know," she whispered. "You just keep our girl safe. That's all I'll ever ask of you."

Gunnar nodded and came back to me. I slid the nine into my belt and took Gunnar's hand. We'd let Vera and Mel move out first. I alone held everyone's secrets. Vera and Melanie's route to tunnels near Bowling Green would take them on a parallel path to Gunnar's and mine for about twenty miles. He might even be able to scent them for part of it. Though, I knew he would never ask me where they were going. They'd hit another set of tunnels about fifteen miles from here. After that, their path would diverge from ours. So, in a sense, none of this felt final to me. Either that, or I'd grown numb from the idea of leaving them.

Gunnar put a steadying hand on my back as we watched Vera and Melanie disappear into the woods. I pushed away the nagging premonition that I'd never see them again. It clawed at me, making it hard to breathe.

TWENTY-SIX

JETT

"**C**ome on," Gunnar said once Melanie and Vera were safely out of sight and scent range. "The sooner we get past Clarksville, the better I'll feel. Vera's right. She knows how to take care of herself and Melanie. Plus, I wouldn't underestimate Mel's strength either. The Pack isn't looking for them. They're looking for me."

"Great," I said, shooting him a narrow-eyed stare. "If that's a pep talk, you suck."

He laughed. "Point taken. Let's get moving in any event. If we stay here much longer, I'm going to start feeling a different urge that will seriously impede our progress for a while."

He gave me swat on the ass that sent a flare of heat through me. Good Lord in heaven, would I ever stop wanting him so much? He took my hand and we started west. Every fiber in my being made me want to go the other way. West led to danger. West led to the patrols.

Gunnar was silent at first. He moved with quick stealth, staying a few paces ahead of me as we made our way through the woods. The plan was to stay along the river for as long as possible. South of Clarksville, we would hit a town called Cedar Ridge. Once Vera and Melanie were safely out of earshot and on their own way, Gunnar told me the Mammoth Forest wolves had some contacts there. It had been years since he himself had been there, but there may just be a chance to find them.

My heart raced with the possibility of sleeping in a real bed tonight. It had been weeks and weeks since I had. Vera and I scoped out abandoned vacation homes along some of the less populated lakes. It was risky because neighbors were usually vigilant. But, when Caro got sicker, we'd taken that chance a few times.

"You're amazing, you know that?" Gunnar said. He took my hand in his. "You're the strongest woman I've ever met. And I've met plenty."

We'd been hiking for two hours at that point. Though it was rough going for me, we kept to the densest part of the wilderness. Gunnar's senses stayed more acute there. I felt an echo of what went through him. Subtle things like a change in the wind, the light staccato of a rabbit's heartbeat two yards away. He processed it all in an instant, making tiny corrections in our path.

"I'm not so strong," I said. "I'm lucky as much as anything else. And I wonder..."

"Wonder what?" he asked, drawing me to him. I had the stamina to keep up with him so far, but I think he sensed my need to break for a moment. We came to a small, bubbling stream and stopped beside it.

"I wonder if some of my luck had to do with fate. Everything aligned in my life to bring me to you. Maybe that wasn't an accident. Fated mates, is that what you called it?"

He smiled. Reaching for me, he took a lock of my hair between his fingers and twirled it. "Yes." His answer rippled through me. "But you've survived because of what's inside of you, not because of me."

I went up on my tiptoes. "And you've survived because of what's inside of you. Gunnar...Camp Hell. We'd watched that place for years. Men don't come out of there. Not whole. Not like you."

He bristled. We hadn't talked about what happened to him there very much. I wasn't sure we ever would. But, it was in him, just like his wolf. I knew his memories haunted his dreams. He murmured in his sleep.

"There were others. Finn, Jones, Rackham. Good men. I'm afraid about what might have happened to them after I left. The Pack knew we were close. If they died in that hellhole because of me..." His voice cracked.

"No," I said. "Don't think it. It's not because of you. It's because of Valent. He's twisted those shifters into something they were never meant to be. I didn't believe that until I met you. I saw what happened to my mother and to Melanie. The Alpha did that, or he made it happen. It's not you. It's not good men like you. This Finn and Rackham and the other one. No matter what, I know they don't blame you for anything they faced after you left. I know they cheered your freedom. So, you have to honor them each day by fighting harder. It's the same way for me. There were twelve of us, Gunnar. Now there's just the three..."

I stopped myself. I couldn't let Caroline's name fall from my lips. I couldn't let my hope for her die.

He pulled me to him. "See? Strongest woman I've ever known. There are strong women in Mammoth Forest too. You can help them."

"How?"

He rested his chin on the top of my head. His strong musk filled my head, making me thrum with desire. "You can teach them how to fight the way you do."

My throat ran dry. It was the closest he'd come to asking me to reveal my last secret. I wanted to, and yet, I wasn't ready. Not yet. Gunnar didn't press. He kissed me, his own lust rising to the surface. Though we both wanted to give in to it, we had to keep moving. We wouldn't be safe until we were underground again.

Gunnar kept looking south. I felt a lump in my throat. Vera and Melanie were only a couple of miles out that way running parallel to us. If Gunnar sensed them, he didn't say anything. If he sensed trouble, I truly didn't know if we would put them in more danger by trying to help or not.

Sweat poured down my back and my stomach growled. I was used to hiking for hours at a time, but Gunnar was harder to keep up with.

"Come on," he said, turning back. "We're on state park lands right now, I think. There should be a real live hiking trail through here somewhere."

I put my hands on the small of my back and stretched. I ached in every joint but didn't want to let on. I could hold my own. "Isn't that dangerous? What if we run into somebody?"

"I'm willing to take the chance. Maybe just for the next hour or so. We'll lose daylight soon. We've made better time than even I thought we would. We'll hit Cedar Ridge first thing in the morning. We've got kind of a signal worked out when we need help. I'm going to find a place to hide you while I run into town and set it off."

My heart flared with alarm. "You mean to tell me you plan on leaving me?"

He came to me, putting a soft kiss on my forehead. I gently pushed him back. There were some things even he couldn't kiss away. "It'll be for an hour, tops. Good chance for you to take a nap. I plan on riding you hard tonight."

I swatted at him as he raised and lowered his brow in a wicked tease. At the same time, my own need grew. "That's what you think. Gunnar, I'm sore in muscles I didn't even know I had."

"Show me which ones," he said, running a hand down my back.

"I'm starving. You talked a big talk up there with Melanie and Vee. You hunt. I'll gather. I saw some blackberry bushes back there. You think it's safe enough to start a small fire?"

"Yeah," he said. "I know I'm right about these being state lands. There's a campground about a mile south of us. I think we can hide in plain sight."

I trusted him. Still, the thought of getting too close to anyone who might report us nagged at me. As much as Gunnar's Mammoth Forest wolves had a network of spies, so did the Pack, and theirs was bigger. But, it became alarmingly clear that if we were to make it to Gunnar's home base, we would need help at some point.

He took my hand and we found the hiking trail. We made

quicker progress now that I didn't have to fight back the brush and gnarled tree branches. Just like Gunnar said, there was a campground in the clearing by a small lake. Mercifully, only three RVs were parked in slots along the water.

"Let *me* go down and fill up the canteens," I said. "You're too big not to be conspicuous. You can start a campfire on that ridge over there. It's far enough away that nobody will be able to really see us, but close enough the smoke won't seem unusual."

"Go quickly," he said. "You're not back up here in ten minutes, I'm coming for you. I don't care who sees me."

"Shh!" I cautioned and pushed him back. "You hunt. I gather. I'm starving."

When I turned to face him, he shifted. The power of it took my breath away as always. Gunnar's great, silver wolf nuzzled my hand and nipped the air. I sank my fingers into the dense fur at the crown of his head. He swished his tail and ran into the forest. At least he'd had the decency to take his jeans off before he let his wolf out. I didn't have any more needle and thread to fix them.

There was a public bathroom next to the boat launch at the lake. Two pickup trucks were parked beside it, but they were empty. Their owners were likely out on the lake. I ducked into the bathroom and checked the bottoms of the stalls.

The coast was clear. I let the cold water run. Stepping back, I caught my reflection in the mirror.

"Ugh," I said, shocked by my appearance. My hair hung wild. It looked like it had grown a foot since I last checked. It hung almost to my waist in thick, black waves. My cheeks had taken on a ruddy color. But, the change in my figure startled me most of all. My body had filled out; I had definition in my biceps. I looked strong, lean, battle-hardened.

The canteens overflowed and I pulled them from the sink, screwing on the caps. The bathroom had a shower stall in one corner. I peered inside. Someone had left travel soaps and shampoo. What I wouldn't give for just five minutes.

Gunnar!

I hadn't tried this before. I reached out with my mind. Had our bond grown so strong that he could hear me?

If you let me take a shower, I'll love you forever. Five minutes. Promise.

I waited. At first, all I could hear was the pounding of my own pulse. Then, slowly, faintly, beneath that, a thought popped into my head. My heart fluttered as I realized it didn't belong to me.

Five minutes. Or I'm coming in after you. Hell, I'm coming in after you anyway.

I staggered away from the sink, startled. Holy shit! I could hear him. He could hear me. He said that might happen eventually, I had no idea it would be this soon.

Peeling off my clothes, I folded them on the wooden bench next to the shower and stepped inside. The water ran quickly hot. I felt like I'd stepped into heaven. I lathered up from head to toe.

You're killing me, you realize that? Touch your nipples. They seem dirty.

"You can feel that?" I gasped. I started to throb between my legs. I did as Gunnar bid, circling my nipples with each index finger. He groaned inside my head.

Oh. Oh. This was new, exciting, and a little scary. I wanted to go to him. My body thrummed with need. I was eager to explore this new power with Gunnar at my side.

I took it slow, throwing my head back, I ran my hand flat over my stomach. Bracing myself against the wall, I slid my fingers between my legs. Gasping, I felt Gunnar's need. His wolf hovered just below the surface, primal, blind with need. I didn't need Gunnar's words in my head to tell me what he wanted. I dipped two fingers inside me. My walls tightened around them. With my other hand, I kneaded my breasts. Water sluiced over me, making me slippery from head to toe.

Gunnar's unspoken command coursed through me. I touched my sex with the tip of my index finger, tracing circles around it until it hardened to a peak.

"Oh," I gasped. Anyone could come in at any time. I smacked my free hand against the wall to steady myself as the rising tide of my orgasm built. I felt Gunnar's breath against my ear. Impossible. He was here but not here. My mark flared hot, matching the pulse beneath my index finger.

I worked myself, sliding my fingers in and out. Gunnar was with me all the way. My knees buckled as I came; the water ran so hot. My body shuddered as I doubled over, thrusting against my own hand as I imagined it was Gunnar.

Soon, baby. Soon. Hurry back to me.

My legs felt weak as I came back into myself. It was time to go.

Rinsing the soap from my body, I squeezed the water from my hair. I hated putting my stale clothes back on a clean body, but there was no help for it right now.

You're a bad influence. I called out to Gunnar. I felt another low growl rumble through me, but he didn't answer.

I slipped on my boots, then gathered my wet hair into a ponytail. It was the best I could do with no towel. With the humidity rising, I'd stay damp for a while. The aftershocks of my orgasm made me tremble as I stepped onto the tile floor. Catching my reflection in the mirror one last time, I smiled. My cheeks were still flushed with unquenched desire.

On my way, I called out again. How quickly I'd gotten used to answering with my mind instead of my voice.

But, Gunnar didn't answer back. I stepped outside. The moon had risen. I looked toward the woods expecting to see Gunnar's campfire. All I saw were the quick flares of a few fireflies. Summer was on the way.

Then, a wall of muscle blocked my path. A flare of alarm went through me as Gunnar finally answered. The echoes of desire faded to terror and my heartbeat ripped through me.

Jett run! Oh, God! Run!

A pair of red eyes flashed and a large black wolf barreled down toward me. He shifted mid-stride and grabbed me by the arm before I could even scream.

TWENTY-SEVEN

GUNNAR

A ble Valent was old. Ancient, really. I'd seen him from a distance during the chaos of battle at Birch Haven. I'd *felt* him ever since in my head, in my bones. Now, I stood face to face with the man.

He stood tall and straight, unlike other men I'd seen his age. Eighty. Maybe even ninety. He had thick, white hair and a full beard. In his prime, he may have been the biggest shifter anyone had ever seen. Even now, he had maybe two inches on my six foot five feet. His eyes flashed from gold to black. My own vision wavered as he walked toward me.

"I've been looking for someone like you for a very long time, Gunnar," he said. His tone was so casual, almost soothing with its dark whiskey timbre and measured cadence.

When I closed my eyes, I could see through Jett's. A black wolf stared her down. There was something familiar about him as his red eyes pierced through her. She tried to go for her weapon, but something made her hesitate. It was *me*. God help her, it was me. My own instincts seem to short-circuit hers. Whatever she'd done to stop the beta wolf the other day, she couldn't do it now. I had to leave her head.

"It hurts, doesn't it?" Able said, walking calmly toward me. The urge to shift burned through me. Instinct told me that was exactly what he wanted.

"Save it, Able," I said. "I'm not going to join you. I know what you are."

I had to stall for time. I had to find a way to let Jett go at least for a moment.

"It's ironic," he said. "Haven't you figured it out yet? Don't you want to know how I found you?"

I did. I'd driven him out of my head. The instant I marked Jett, she gave me the strength to break the hold the Pack had on me for good. And yet, as soon as I thought it, Able's eyes flashed with menace. He couldn't read my mind. I *knew* he couldn't. Still, he looked at me as if he knew everything I was thinking.

"Gunnar, I know more about shifters than any living soul. I know what drives you. What you fear. What you need. You're an Alpha. You were born to lead. It's clouded your judgment this whole time and you can't even see it. You can't protect her. You never could."

"Maybe she doesn't need me to protect her. She's been doing a damn good job of it all by herself." My fear for Jett exploded inside of me. At the same time, pride filled me. She was strong. She'd faced down the Pack before.

Kill him! I shouted to her with my mind.

My vision shifted from Able standing before me, to what Jett saw. She stood stock still, her fingers playing over the handle of her weapon. Could she outdraw him? She was looking for something in his eyes. It held the secret to how she'd killed the red wolf and got the jump on Lowell. But, this one was different. He was familiar somehow. She knew him.

A hand on my shoulder. Her shoulder. I couldn't sort out what she saw from what I did. Able closed in.

"You think you can kill me if you're strong enough," Able said. "You can't. None of you can. Do you know how many have tried?"

"Why don't you just do it and get it over with?" I said. "You know you can't subjugate me. You would have done it already if you could. You're old and fading."

Able's eyes flared red and he charged at me. My knees buckled with the urge to shift. I held my ground. Something told me if I gave in to my baser instincts now, he could break me.

Jett started to panic. I dug my fingers into the bark of the oak tree beside me, gripping it hard enough to draw blood. A hand slid to the back of my neck. No, not my neck. It was Jett's. The black wolf had shifted. His red eyes still beamed with menace; he pulled her to him, tilting her face up to his. I closed my eyes, but I couldn't see it. His face was a blur to me. But, his skin burned a path over her flesh as he ran a thumb along her jaw. She recoiled from it. So did I.

"Careful," Able said. "You wouldn't want to make any sudden movements that Sutter might take as a threat."

Sutter. My old friend. My betrayer. Memories slammed into place. I outran him. He could never keep up. When he shifted, it was clumsy, slow, ungainly. He was a beta. I knew it then; so did he. I thought I spared his feelings by not mentioning it. I told him lies about how I could help him get better control of his wolf. I couldn't. Only his Alpha could.

Pain blossomed in my chest. Blow after blow sent me spiraling down. He thought he could break me. I focused on the dank smell of rotted branches. They curled far beneath my feet in the soft earth. I imagined making myself so small I could slip through the cracks in the concrete floor. Anything to free me from Maestro's next blow.

Maestro. Sutter. I couldn't see him. I could never see him. I could only smell cold dirt and rotted pine. The dragonsteel chains chaffed my wrists and the filthy rag around my eyes was tied so tight my head throbbed.

Look who's winning now, Gunnar. Maestro's thick whisper and fetid breath wafted in front of my face.

I was right back there. Camp Hell. Had it always been this way? Was all of it a trick of the mind? Jett. My freedom. Had I dreamt it all?

His fingers curled around my throat, pressing my windpipe. He shouldn't be strong enough to break me. He could *never* be as strong as I was, and that's why he hated me.

My eyes snapped open and the blindfold fell away. No. This wasn't my vision, it was Jett's. Maestro's hands closed around her throat as he pulled her off her feet.

Maestro. Sutter. They were one in the same. How had I not sensed it before?

"Ah, you remember now," Able said. I staggered backward as reality slammed back into my chest. Maestro was Sutter. Sutter had his hands around Jett's throat and she was paralyzed by it because of me. *My* thoughts, my memories churned in her mind. My connection to her would be the very thing that could get her killed.

"You've been waiting," I said, though my voice didn't sound like my own. "All this time, you knew if I claimed my mate, it would break your hold, but it would make me easier to track."

"Gunnar, I told you. No one alive knows shifters more than I do. I'm not just an Alpha, my son. I'm *the* Alpha. What did you think would happen?"

"No," I staggered back. No. No. It couldn't happen. I would never let it happen. I closed my mind to him. I closed my mind to her.

"She's magnificent," Able said. "I had someone special in mind for her. Did she tell you that? Maybe she didn't know."

"It's over," I said. "Your little Birch Haven experiment is finished. You want to punish me, punish me. You don't need Jett to do it."

I reached out with my mind, drawing on strength I hadn't tapped before. If my connection to Jett was one strand, maybe Able's connection to me was another. Maybe I could use it against him.

"She's strong," he said. "She might even be the one. I think it's worth a try."

The one? I tried to build a wall in my mind. Let Jett be Jett. Let her fight. Sutter put her down. That meant something. At the same time, I felt Able reaching out, pushing at the corners of my mind.

"I could let you have her," Able said. "I could let her live. That's up to you."

"No!" I said, pushing back. Able rounded on me. I held my ground. Don't shift. Don't shift. Don't shift.

"Submit to me as your Alpha and I'll let you keep Jett as your mate. It's the best deal you'll ever get and one I won't make again."

I staggered sideways. Able's power turned my stomach. He was so strong. Buzzing, like a thousand locusts, bored through my mind. He tested for weaknesses. Images of my mother flashed before me. Sutter. The last day when Able's soldiers came for me, accusing me of turning traitor. The day I chose to run rather than submit. The day I met Liam and Mac. Molly's smiling face as she bound one of my wounds. Jett. Always Jett. He would use it all against me.

"Your choice," Able said, as he felt my will. I would never willingly submit to him, even if it cost me my life. "Such a waste she'll be. Maybe I'll let Sutter have her for a while. He deserves some R and R."

My wolf sprang free. I couldn't hold the shift back any longer. The world grew brighter as my wolf eyes locked on Able. He crouched low, but stayed human. His pull on my mind stretched taut. Just a thin membrane of resistance separated me from chaos. It's what he wanted. It's how he knew he could win.

Gunnar! Jett's mental cry tore at me. She felt the walls weakening around me. I snapped my jaw then let a howl rip from me. I closed her off. This began and ended with Able and me.

I launched myself at him. Able shifted. His wolf loomed large and silver in front of me. His eyes went blood-red and I lost my footing. Oh, God. His hold was strong indeed.

But, he was holding on only to me!

As Able lunged for me, sinking his knife-like fangs into my neck, his hold broke on Sutter. I saw it happen through Jett's eyes. Sutter took a staggering step backward as my blood filled Able's mouth. He dropped low and shifted. Sutter's wolf eyes flashed gold then faded to amber. It was just an instant, but Jett's pulse pounded. It meant something to her.

Able released his grip. I rolled away and got back to my feet. Before he could strike again, I hurled my body into his flank, throwing him end over end. He rounded quickly, spreading his paws wide and dropping his head low. His threatening snarl echoed off the trees. I felt his intention change. He no longer wanted to subjugate me. He wanted to kill me.

I felt Jett's fingers close around the cold handle of her nine. Sutter's eyes were still a dull amber, his movements lumbering. It all happened in a split second. Able dropped his head low. Sutter's eyes changed again, glowing red. But an instant before, Jett got her shot off. It ripped through Sutter's chest, spinning him hard to the left.

Able yelped as he felt Sutter's pain. It was just a moment. A rift in the fiber that held Able to Sutter. It was all I needed. I leaped through the air and sank my teeth into Able's neck.

He was just a wolf. Just an ancient, strong wolf. I was stronger. Able's eyes widened in shock as he realized what I understood. Blood poured from the puncture wounds I'd made in his chest. Able kicked off with his feet, sending me sailing through the air. I landed hard, my spine crunching against a tree. Adrenaline fueled me and I popped up. Able did too. He panted hard, foam dripping from his fangs. Sweat and blood matted his fur. But, he kept on coming.

Mortal. He could be killed. I saw the light fade from his eyes and his scent changed, colored by fear. He wasn't used to it. His death was mine. My Alpha rose strong.

Submit! The command filled my head, but it was mine, not Able's. Ancient instinct fueled me. I was stronger, younger, virile. He was old, weakening. It was always supposed to be this way. Old Alphas fall; others rise. New packs form. Even now, I could sense Able's instincts flaring hot. It was in his blood to give in to me; my nature called to his. Succession. Strength. Change. It was how packs had survived for millennia.

But Able Valent was no ordinary Alpha. Nature did not matter to him. He was a *Tyrannous Alpha* and one blow from me, no matter how devastating, would not change him.

Jett's scream filled the air, searing through my heart like a dagger. My vision clouded and I swayed on my feet. The pain from Able's bite tore through me at last; blood leached from me.

Sutter was mortally wounded, but his heart still beat. He would use the last gasps of life to do Able's bidding. My ears pricked as dozens of other wolves poured down the hill. The Pack. The instant their Alpha's blood began to flow, he called to them. Mindless. Murderous. Jett wasn't safe.

Sutter made his move. He leaped into the air and caught Jett's right arm in his jaws. At full strength, he could have torn it off. The effort of it made his legs give out. Jett dropped the gun. Sutter was on her. In another instant, he would tear her open.

Able was two feet from me, his strength still fading. He was weak, but he would not be easy to kill. A life for a life. Jett's or Able's. One Alpha versus another.

I gave in to my nature. With each beat of my heart, I knew where I belonged. I covered the distance in seconds. My paws left the ground. Arcing high, I landed on Sutter's back. The weight of me crushed his spine. He released his death grip on Jett's arm. She was stunned, gravely injured, but she rolled away.

Fueled by his own survival instinct and his master's will, Sutter got to his feet. The ground was stained red from his blood. I went in for the kill. Sutter staggered backward as I tore open his throat. He had nothing left to bleed. His red eyes faded to amber, then to gold, then finally to a deep brown as he shifted back in death. His broken body curled in on itself. His lips were moving as he tried to say his dying words. But, I would not be his audience. The Maestro was finished.

"Gunnar!" Jett cried. "The Pack!"

Scores of wolves poured down from the hill. Half broke off, heading for their fallen leader. But, the others came straight for us.

Jett got to her feet. She was bleeding badly from the wound on her arm. She wouldn't die. I would not let her die. There was no time to ask her if she could run.

Grab on to me! I shouted to her with my mind. *Whatever happens, don't let go!*

Jett gave me a desperate nod. She wrapped her good arm around my neck and hoisted herself on my back. The blood from my own wound coated us both, but it didn't matter. Jett was alive and so was I. If we had any hope of staying that way, I'd have to outrun the Pack.

TWENTY-EIGHT

JETT

No pain. No breath. No sight.

Gunnar covered the ground on powerful legs. His muscles hardened to steel as we flew west. I sensed the Pack through him. They were beyond reason, fueled only by murderous rage and their Alpha's command. Mindless. Soulless. In some part of me, I felt sympathy for them. Once, they'd been just like Gunnar or the men who served with him, hadn't they? Were those men still in there, or had Able Valent's hold broken what was human about them?

So much sorrow. So much rage. It blinded them. I could feel it. As Gunnar's blood mixed with mine, the Alpha's greatest crime unfurled before me. It left me breathless, weightless.

We reached the outskirts of Gordon City. The town blinked to life in front of us. To the east, the highway loomed. Gunnar headed that way. Panic flared through me. We were safer in the shadows. We'd survived staying away from large groups of people where the Pack could blend in and hide. Now, we were charging straight for it.

There was an industrial complex at the very edge of town. The smokestacks of a large oil refinery loomed. Its sprawling parking lot held hundreds of cars. Gunnar broke off and ran for it. The third shift was just letting out as the first shift rolled in. I knew Gunnar's mind even if he couldn't transmit it to me.

I slid off Gunnar's back. He stayed in his wolf. He was fierce and deadly, blood matting his fur. His silver wolf eyes gleamed brightly in the dim light.

"What the fuck?" One of the factory workers had the ill luck to walk straight into our path. His overalls were covered in grease and held a lunch pail against his chest almost like a shield. I turned to him.

"Your keys," I said. "I just need your keys."

"You outta your mind, lady?"

Gunnar dropped his head. His murderous growl vibrated through me. The worker dropped his empty pail to the ground and put his hands up. "Get away from him," he said to me. "Walk slow."

"Your keys," I said again. "Nobody's going to hurt you."

He tossed them to me. I supposed now I could add grand theft auto to my list of crimes. I can't imagine what I looked like to him. My entire right side was covered in blood. It hurt, but I knew shock and adrenaline drove me. I took his keys and hit the lock button. The lights of a silver F-250 flared three cars down. Gunnar went for it.

He shifted on a dime and slid into the driver's seat. I looked back at the truck's owner. He was older, probably close to retirement. With his jaw on the ground, he shook his head and put his hands up, backing away. I shrugged and forced a smile.

"I'm sorry," I said. "You'll get it back." I don't know why I said it, but it made me feel better. Gunnar laid on the horn and I ran for the passenger seat.

Climbing in, I barely got the door shut before Gunnar slammed the truck into reverse and peeled out of the parking space. He blew through the stop sign and headed for the highway.

"They're still coming!" I gasped. I reached for my nine and realized with horror I didn't have it anymore. In all the excitement, I'd dropped it to the ground next to Sutter, the wolf I killed. When his name burned through Gunnar, I knew it too.

"Don't worry about it," he said. "If the Pack gets within firing range, we'll be dead already. There's too many of them."

He was right. We hit the on-ramp at nearly a hundred miles an hour. I chanced a look behind us. Dozens of pairs of glowing red eyes wavered in the distance. There were woods on either side of the road. They were coming from everywhere. Gunnar pressed the gas even harder. The truck lurched in protest, but responded. He took it to top speed, nearly one hundred and ten.

"Just don't fall apart on me now," Gunnar whispered. I wasn't sure if he meant me or the truck. Probably both.

"We should go south," I said, my voice cracking. "Hit the border, once and for all."

"No," Gunnar said. His words came out in a hiss of pain. The truck had an extended cab. I leaned over the seat. I found a few old t-shirts, rags, spare work clothes. The poor guy who owned it looked like he slept it in regularly. Quickly stripping the rags, I pressed one to the wound in Gunnar's side. It had stopped bleeding, but the edges were raw and open.

"Don't worry about me," he said. "Use those for you. Can you wrap your arm tight? There'll be help where we going. If I can get us there before they catch up."

I lurched to the side as Gunnar weaved around slower vehicles. It earned us a chorus of angry honks in our wake. Gunnar kept on going. With each mile marker, my heart started to ease. I could still see the glowing eyes in the distance, but they were fading.

"When we get close enough, we're going to have to ditch the truck," he said. "Baby, can you hang on a little while longer? I know you're in pain."

My voice caught in my throat. I held back the tears I'd wanted to cry since the moment I felt Able Valent's hold on Gunnar return. I thought I'd lost him. I *felt* his pain when he realized who the black wolf was. Sutter, his betrayer. Maestro, his torturer. And yet, he'd held strong. He'd fought it all back for me. We'd done it together. My strength was Gunnar's strength.

"I can go as far as you can go," I said, putting a gentle hand on his arm. He flicked his eyes to me, then focused on the road. His jaw jumped as he clenched it. I felt his own heart thump with emotion. So close. I'd been so close to losing him.

We sat in silence as the road stretched ahead of us. Each howl in the distance cut through me. But, they faded. Each time I looked back, I saw fewer eyes. Five miles from Cave City, they faded to nothing.

Suddenly, Gunnar pulled to the shoulder. His headlights shone on an exit sign. Shadow Springs. My heart soared.

"Come on," he said. "We have to go the rest of the way on foot. I'll carry you if you're not strong enough."

"They're not here," I said. "I don't feel the Pack."

Gunnar pulled me to him, kissing my forehead. "We just might make it."

"Don't say that," I told him. "You'll jinx us."

Smiling, Gunnar opened the driver's side door. When I reached to open mine, pain exploded through me. Gunnar's eyes widened with alarm and he pulled me out of the cab. I tried to stand, but my legs gave out.

He reached into the back of the truck. He found one clean jumpsuit and put it on. Then, he tucked his arm beneath my legs and lifted me. "Come on," he said. "It's not far. You'll make it."

I tried to smile, but it hurt too much. The ground became a blur beneath me as Gunnar started to run. We took to the woods again where I knew he belonged. With each step, new strength poured through him.

Home. Friends. His hope bled through me.

Then, my heart dropped as a menacing howl rent the air. One of the largest wolves I'd ever seen blocked our path to the woods. His mighty jaws snapped and his back went up, ready to pounce for the kill. His red fur bristled and he pawed the ground in a clear challenge.

"Gunnar!" I yelled. Gunnar put himself between the wolf and me. Gold eyes narrowed and gleamed as he came toward us. Behind him, the woods drew dense. Could we make a run for it? I pulled on Gunnar's sleeve. Strong as he was, I knew he wasn't physically ready for another fight so soon. And this wolf looked ready to tear him to shreds.

Gunnar pulled away from me. I felt his heart thundering through me. He went to the wolf. The wolf bared his fangs and snarled.

"Gunnar, no," I said. My hand went reflexively for the gun I no longer carried. I knew he'd rather die than submit to the Pack. Please, God, don't let that be his plan now.

Gunnar dropped low, meeting the red wolf's eyes. Then, he reached forward and grabbed his head. His shoulders shook as deep laughter erupted from him. The wolf snapped his jaw but only in the air. He pushed Gunnar sideways, nearly knocking him off the ground. Then, he let out a whine and shook his great head while Gunnar regained his balance and threw his arms around the wolf in an embrace.

"Jett," he said, laughing. "Meet Liam. Liam, this is Jett."

Liam's wolf chuffed a greeting as Gunnar let him go. Liam came to me, tail high. The top of his head came up to my shoulders. He stared at me with intelligent, golden eyes. He raised his head once then brought it down in a sort of wolf nod.

"Come on," Gunnar said. "We need to get underground. Liam, we need Molly. Fast."

Liam's wolf let out a short yip and he swung his head to the side. I didn't speak wolf by any means, but this seemed like an invitation. Smiling, Gunnar took my hand. All the tension of that last few hours seemed to drain from him. With each step he took deeper into the woods, he seemed stronger, taller. Relief bled through me as I squeezed Gunnar's hand.

Liam's wolf followed, but kept his distance. I knew instinctively he was watching out for us. If we hadn't thrown off the Pack, he'd have to sound an alarm. Out here alone, he put himself at great risk. I didn't know him. I hadn't even met the man inside of him. Already, I liked him immensely.

Gunnar stopped when we reached a clump of dead branches. He pushed them aside to reveal a hole in the ground. "Come on," he said. "Duck when you pass through. And stick close to me. There's a steep drop off on your left side as we go down. After that, it's not so dangerous."

Nodding, I followed his lead. My head grew light as the effects of my injury started to catch up with me. Gunnar sensed it right away and wrapped his arm around me. I pushed back. I'd come this far. I wanted the Mammoth Forest wolves to see me walk in on my own power. It mattered to me somehow.

Gunnar's brow furrowed with concern. But he didn't try to pick me up. The cavern entrance was just as he said. Still, it was a damn sight easier to traverse than the tunnels. Hell, it was a palace compared to what I was used to. When we reached the end of the first descending pathway, we walked into a larger, round cavern, reminding me of a rotunda.

LED lights flared bright and my spine prickled. We weren't alone. A man and woman waited to greet us arm in arm. He was just as huge as Gunnar was with broad shoulders and well-muscled biceps and forearms. His t-shirt stretched taut over a massive chest. He kept a protective hand on the woman's back. She was blonde with kind eyes that shone as she looked up at her man. She was also heavily pregnant.

Another woman came rushing through another passageway to the left of us. She was short, with brown hair pulled into a ponytail. She wore green hospital scrubs and wiped her hands on a towel as she rushed past the other couple.

"Gunnar!" she gushed. "My God, let me look at you!"

Gunnar went into her waiting arms. As she hugged him, she looked over his shoulder at me, her wide brown eyes twinkling with tears.

"Molly," he said. "This is Jett. She's hurt. One of Able's wolves took a bite out of her arm. It's bad."

I tried to play it off, but my legs turned to rubber as I stood there. Molly rushed forward and slid her arm around my waist. "Whoa," she said. "I've got you. Come on. Let's see how bad is."

Gunnar was at my side. This time, I didn't have the strength to protest when he swept me off my feet. He followed Molly out of the main cavern, down a passageway, and into a smaller cave. I marveled at this one. Well-lit with strings of LED lights on the floor and ceilings, it had four hospital beds and shelving with medical supplies. Except for the cave walls, it could be a real doctor's office.

Molly made quick work of examining me. She cleaned the wound and hooked me up to an IV "You're strong," she said, smiling. "And probably pretty brave. And this looks worse than it is. It'll scar something awful, but it's superficial. You hear me, Gunnar? I'll clean it, stitch it, and I think maybe a course of antibiotics wouldn't go to waste. You did good. You got her here in time. Understand?"

I hadn't noticed, but Gunnar's eyes had stayed silver since we came into the cave. Now, they dimmed, turning to their normal blue. It appeared this Molly knew him well indeed.

I reached out and took Gunnar's hand. "It's okay," I said. "I'm going to be okay. And so are you. Now go catch up with your friends. I have a feeling everyone's got a lot of questions."

"She's right," Molly said. She put a light hand on Gunnar's arm and shot me a wink. "And I suppose you have plenty of questions yourself. I'll answer the first one and the only one that matters, Jett. You're home now. And you're among friends."

Relief flooded through me. It was that and the loss of blood. I sank back against the pillows and closed my eyes, feeling safe for the first time in years.

TWENTY-NINE

GUNNAR

Anyone who didn't know me might think I had more tiger inside of me than wolf. I paced outside the medical cavern. Liam and Mac barred my entry. If I wasn't confident Molly could take care of Jett, even they wouldn't be strong enough to stop me. As it was, I had the urge to rip their knowing smiles from their faces. At the same time, I'd never been more glad to see two people in my life.

Finally, Molly emerged. She put a hand on Liam's shoulder. He and Mac moved to let her through. Her bloodstained scrubs sent a spear of terror through me, but her soft smile kept me from losing it.

"She's going to be all right," Molly said. "You got her to me in time."

I deflated with relief. As the weight of my fear left me, my legs went. I staggered back, gripping the wall for support. I sank down, hands over my face. Liam and Mac came to me.

"Come on," Mac said. "We've got a lot to talk about."

"Later," I said. "I need to be with Jett."

"It's okay," Molly said. She squatted down so we were eye to eye. Her brow furrowed with worry as she touched my cheek then pulled my shirt away.

"I'm fine," I said. "It's already starting to heal."

"Hmm. You still need stitching. That's a wolf bite. You know damn well you'd have been better off with just a simple gunshot, Gunnar. Let me do my job."

"Later," I said again. "I mean it. I'm okay."

"And so is your Jett. She's something fierce, all right. I think I'm going to like her. But, she needs rest and no more excitement for the next twenty-four hours or so. I'm still a little worried about infection, but it's nothing I won't be able to tackle. You did good, Gunnar. You protected your mate."

Her eyes twinkled with mischief as she patted my shoulder. Liam held a hand out to her. She grasped it and rose to her feet. I ran a hard hand over my jaw and did the same.

"I promise," Molly said. "The minute her eyelids so much as flutter, I'll come get you. You'll be the first face she sees when she wakes up. Don't be surprised if that takes a while. She looks like she hasn't had a decent night's sleep in years."

"She hasn't," I said, my tone solemn. "She's been on the run, living in tunnels. She's lost..."

Molly put a hand on my chest. "She's safe, Gunnar. So are you." Molly's eyes misted with tears. I realized she'd been running on her own adrenaline since the minute I got back. I'd been so caught up with worry for Jett, I hadn't stopped to consider how much Molly and the others might have worried about me.

Molly gave a choked cry. I pulled her to me and hugged her. "It's okay, Moll. I'm okay. I'm back."

She snorted hard, ruining my shirt. Liam had a gentle hand on her back. His wolf eyes went gold.

"Don't you ever do that again," Molly said. She ran a sleeve under her eyes and stepped back into Liam's arms. "You scared the hell out of me."

"I'll try not to," I said.

"Go, shoo," she said, gesturing. "You boys have a lot of catching up to do and decisions to make. I'll watch over Jett. Promise."

"Thanks," said. I hugged Molly again. Then, I locked eyes with Liam over her head. She was right. We had a lot to talk about.

The three of us went into the main rotunda. It was quiet there for now. Payne and Jagger were missing. I was almost afraid to ask where they were. When I turned to Mac and Liam, I found I didn't quite know where to start.

"God," Mac said. "It's good to have you back, man." He came to me, slapping me on the back as we embraced. "We thought for sure you were dead until...Jagger."

Liam put a hand on Mac's shoulder. A quick look passed between them. There was something they weren't telling me. I didn't like it one bit. For now though, I knew there was something bigger at stake.

"I almost killed him," I said, starting at the most important part. "I had Able in my sights. He was wounded...bad. He tried to control me, but he couldn't. I think that's the secret he's trying to hide from the rest of the Pack. He's so old. I've never seen an Alpha still in control who's as old as he is. I pushed back. He couldn't break me. I swear to God I was about to break him. I had to let go. I had to go after Jett."

I sat on a boulder, resting my hands on my knees.

"It's okay," Liam said. I hadn't realized until just that moment how much I needed one of them to say that. "We're the last two people you have to explain or justify the choice you made. Because there was no choice. Jett's your mate. She would have died if you hadn't gone to her."

Nodding, I threaded my hands through my hair, half wanting to tear it out. "He can be beaten though. If we can get him alone again, I swear it. It's why we're such a threat to him. He kills Alphas because he knows he can't control them in the same way as the betas. We're a threat. And it's also why he knew I'd be no good to him if he *did* fully subjugate me. I think it would have turned my mind to mush. He wanted my intel about the rest of you and where we're hiding. He didn't get it though. I swear to you. My Alpha's too strong. I would have died before telling him anything or leading the Pack here."

"That was never a concern," Mac said. He had a hand on my shoulder. "Not once."

"Where's Payne?" I asked.

"Gone," Liam answered abruptly. "Ever since Birch Haven, he's been AWOL a lot. He won't admit it, but being that close to Valent churned up some stuff in him. So, he's been doing a lot of recon. He's run some friends to the border and back. I don't think he's spent the night in the caves once since you...went missing."

I sat back. "I get it," I said. "You think he doesn't trust himself?"

Mac sighed and sat on another bolder a few feet from me. "I think he's just trying to work some shit out. We've given him some space. After everything with Jagger...the last thing I wanna do is mess with his head."

"He's no better?" I asked. Jagger had been damn near catatonic since losing his mate, Keara over a year ago. It took a minute for me to let that settle in. I now understood how devastating that had to have been for him. I couldn't even bring myself to think about how I'd feel if something really had happened to Jett. It's a wonder he was still alive. I'd been gone so long. Six long months.

A silence fell between us. There was something Mac and Liam didn't want to tell me. I closed my eyes and let out a hard breath. "Don't tell me," I said. We'd worried for months that Jagger might actually try to take his own life. His despair over losing Keara seemed to have physical weight. It crushed him, suspending him in some unreachable place between his wolf and the man he once was. Molly had been the only one with true hope where Jagger was concerned.

"He's better in a sense," Liam said. "You should go see him. He took your loss pretty hard too."

"You didn't lose me," I rose. I put my hand out, clasping it with Liam's. "I'm too fucking stubborn for that. But why didn't you guys warn me what it would be like?"

Liam and I broke. Mac stood there dumbfounded, then the two of them burst into laughter. "You mean Jett? Man, there's no way words would have been enough for that. How the hell did you find her after everything you went through?"

I told them a little about what it was like in Camp Hell. The deepest truth was something no man could understand unless he'd lived it. I think Mac and Liam got that. They didn't pry. But, the part I *did* want to share, I did with a huge smile on my face.

"She was the one who busted me out. She's from Birch Haven. When she wakes up, she's going to have a ton of questions. There's a girl in particular she's been trying to find. Jett is...well...when you get the chance to get to know her, you'll see what I mean."

"We already do, brother," Liam said. "We can see it in your eyes. She was meant for you. Which means she's going to be something pretty special. And you know it means we'll protect her with our lives too if it comes to it."

My throat clogged with emotion. I'd been alone so long, I'd almost forgotten what it was like to have men I could count on. It made my heart ache that much more for Jagger.

And then, as if I'd conjured him, he appeared at the cavern entrance standing tall and stoic, his face hard and his eyes dark.

"Jagger," I whispered. His body was ravaged with new scars cutting a web-like pattern across his chest. Only wolf claws did that. The skin around his wrists was rough and calloused where he'd worn his own dragonsteel chains. In his case, we'd done it to protect him. Having spent months in them myself as a prisoner, I knew Jagger wouldn't have seen much of a difference.

Jagger's eyes flicked to Mac and Liam. He didn't say a word. He straightened his back and entered the cavern. Pain etched his face. Losing Keara had left him gutted, hollowed out. But today, he was on his feet. My heart flooded with a dozen emotions as he came to me.

"It's good to see you," I said. I put a hand on his shoulder. He tensed up, but didn't pull away. I took his hand, clasping it like I'd just done with Liam. His eyes darted back and forth over mine. His lips pursed, but he didn't say anything. It was as if the words were still trapped inside. The agony of his heart was written in the deep lines near his eyes and his gaunt cheeks.

"It's okay," I said, letting him go. "I'm okay."

His nostrils flared and he gave me a slight nod, but that was all he could muster. Give it time, I thought. He's come this far.

Jagger stepped away and jerked his chin toward Mac and Liam. "We'll take care of it," Liam said. Jagger dropped his head and walked back out of the cavern.

For a moment, I couldn't breathe. I knew how big a step that was for Jagger to make. I ran a hand over my jaw. "Wow," was all I could find to say. "He's...that was..."

"Progress," Mac finished. "It was. But there's something you need to know. Follow us."

When I shot a questioning look at Liam, he merely turned and followed Mac out. Heart pounding with new fear, I fell in step behind them. They led me deeper into the caves. Before I left, we'd started clearing out new caverns. After taking out the Shadow Springs general, we had more and more refugees to house. It unsettled me that most of these new caverns were empty. I wasn't sure if that was good or bad news. We came to the last one before the passageway was blocked. My inner wolf pricked as a familiar scent filled my head.

No. It couldn't be!

I practically shoved Mac and Liam out of the way. My step faltered as I burst into the cavern. Bright eyes glinted, adjusting to the light. There, against the wall sitting on a rocky ledge was Finn. He greeted me with a broad smile and a choked cry as he realized it was me.

"Gunnar!" Finn leaped to his feet and came to me. He launched himself at me. Slapping his back, I hugged him. He was thin and frail, but so much stronger than the last time I saw him. I hadn't dared to hope. My heart soared with relief.

"How?" I asked, pulling him back by the shoulders. My face split into a wide grin as I looked over his shoulder. Rackham and Jones sat against the wall. They were more cautious, preferring to watch Finn with me. I understood. We'd never been close like Finn and me. And I didn't know what horrors befell them after I broke free.

"It was a fucking miracle is what," Finn said. "Oh, we all caught holy hell after you left. But, the guards went nuts. The Alpha came down hard on 'em. But then he left to find you. He gave orders to either kill or subjugate all three of us. Maestro's choice." Finn's voice cracked on the name.

"It's okay," I said, still gripping his shoulders. I met him eye to eye. "Listen to me, Finn. He's gone. You hear me, man? Maestro's dead. It's a long fucking story, but I tore him to bits and watched him die. He's gone for good."

A single tear fell down Finn's cheek. For an instant, I wanted the ground to open up and swallow me. It was my fault. These men had been punished for information about me they didn't have. He wasn't Maestro to me anymore. He was Sutter. It tore at me to think any action he took against Finn and the others was made worse because of me.

"You sure?" This from Rackham.

"I'm sure. He's dead." I lifted my shirt to show them the now healing wound I bore from Sutter's bite. "Gave me this as a parting gift. But he's gone."

"Thank you," Finn said. He stepped out of my grip, his eyes glinting with tears. "All of you. If that crazy motherfucker hadn't come when he did, they were going to kill us. That's if we were lucky. I still don't know how he did it. Gunnar, you should have seen him. Dude came down like an avalanche, all silver-eyed fury. He took out three guards in seconds. They threw everything they had at him, tore him to bits, but he just kept on coming. I'll never forget it."

My head swirled with Finn's words. I looked back at Mac and Liam. Understanding slammed into place. The motherfucker in question was Jagger. I'd just seen the new scars over his body.

"We'll catch up later," I said. "I gotta check in on my girl. You have everything you need here?"

Jones and Rackham nodded. Finn stepped back and joined them. "This is heaven," Finn answered. "Sweet, sweet heaven. You know, I thought you were crazy. I thought those were fever dreams you had, talkin' about her jet-black hair and luscious tits."

A protective growl escaped from me. It earned me a nervous laugh and Finn's hands thrown up in surrender. But, he winked and smiled. "You go to her," he said. "And tell her thank you. I know she had a part in this."

"I will," I said, reaching to shake Finn's hand again. "I'll be back. Promise."

Finn shook his head and disbelief. The three of them looked

awful, but they were whole. Time might just bring them back all
the way.

I left the cavern with Mac and Liam. New questions swirled in
my mind. As we made our way back toward the infirmary, Liam
started to answer them.

"Payne's the one who figured out where they'd taken you. It's
one of the reasons he's spent so much time away. He's been
strengthening our contacts, gathering intel. He got word of the
prison camp. It wasn't confirmed, but he heard a rumor there
was a prisoner the Alpha had taken a special interest in.
Someone mentioned the tattoo on your chest and we figured we
were on to something. We were starting to hash out a rescue
plan. Then Jagger..."

"He just took off," Mac picked up the story. "Molly was the one
who put it together where he was going. She'd seen some signs
that troubled her. Gunnar, I don't think Jagger ever meant to
come back. He was on a suicide mission."

I stopped and leaned hard against the cave wall. "Christ. Do
you realize how close he probably came to getting his wish? It
had to be dumb luck and brute strength on his side. That's all."

"Obviously, you were already gone when he got there. He could
have left, but he didn't. He set those men free and brought them
back. Or rather, they dragged him back here. Molly almost
didn't get to him in time. She won't admit it, but he begged her
to let him die. We all heard it. He hasn't talked since."

"Shit," I said. "It's really that bad?"

Liam nodded. "He's been calm for the last few days
since. But..."

"But he might try something even more dangerous the next

time," I said. "Shit. I can't pretend I'm not grateful for what he tried to do for me...and for Finn and the others, but..."

"But, yeah," Mac said. "Now you're where we are."

"Listen," I said. "He's come this far. When I left, he was barely eating and bashing his head against the wall if we didn't chain him. Now, at least he can fight for something. I've seen men survive things you can't imagine. Let's not lose hope."

"Oh, nobody's losing hope," Molly's bright voice reached us as she stepped out of the shadows. She stood with her hands on her hips. "Not on my watch. Speaking of that, Jett's waking up."

I tried to brush past Molly. She put a flat palm on my chest to stop me. "You're going to let me tend to that bite before you take another step, mister. That's an order."

"Yeah?" I teased. "Who's going to hold me down so you can?"

No sooner had I said it before Liam and Mac grabbed me forcefully by the arms, their inner wolves growling a threat.

"Fine," I laughed. "I suppose I can't fight off all three of you."

"Damn straight you can't," Molly said. "Let's get you cleaned up and presentable. I've only just met her, but I have a hunch your Jett is worth all the fuss."

My heart soaring, I went with them down to the infirmary.

THIRTY

Jett

"Hold still!" I commanded. "And quit scratching. You're going to rip those stitches out!"

Gunnar and I were a pair. I had my arm in a sling, my own stitches itching like the devil. Molly had bandaged his waist. It had been three days and she told me he could take them out today. We'd both threatened to throw him back in dragonsteel if he tried to rip them out before that.

"You're just as bad as she is," he growled.

"That's right," I said. "Which means you know you're gonna lose this fight, wolfman. Now let me see."

He let out a defeated sigh and I started to unwrap the bandages. Molly wanted to be here, but she'd been called away.

"You want me to sit on him?" A wry voice echoed down the passageway. Gunnar and I had claimed what I now called our suite. We stayed in a group of caverns branching east from the main rotunda. Eve and Mac stayed just across the way. Further down the hall, Eve had shown me the crown jewel of the hidden Mammoth Cave system. Steaming hot springs bubbled up just below the main rooms. After today, Gunnar had the all clear to submerge himself. My heart came alive with possibilities. Gunnar, of course, knew my mind well enough now to feel my need instantly.

"You'll crush my ribs, woman," Gunnar teased. Eve came to the archway, standing with her hands at the small of her back. Her stomach bulged as the life within it swelled and rolled.

Eve was a marvel to me. Mac's mate, she was the reason Birch Haven fell. On my second night here in the caves, she'd come to talk to me. Her warm smile put me at ease. I couldn't stop staring at her stomach. She took me into her confidence that night, placing my hand where her belly curved. She held it firm and after a moment, I felt the mysterious magic of the small baby inside of her. He turned, kicking out one limb and I knew him instantly for what he was.

"They say he'll be an Alpha, just like his daddy," Eve whispered. Her tone held joy and fear all at once. I suppose every new mother feels that way. I couldn't help but bring my hand to my own empty womb. Would Gunnar and I be brave enough to fill it someday? I secretly hoped so.

Gunnar knew Eve and I had been putting off a conversation for a few days. "Go," he said. "This can wait. I'll meet you both in the main rotunda. If I haven't found Molly before that, you can have the honor of taking these damn stitches out yourself."

I wagged a finger at him. "That better be a promise not to touch them, mister." He rolled his eyes but gave me a half-hearted salute.

Then, Eve and I walked down the dark cave passageways together. She held a lantern in front of her and we cast ghostly shadows on the walls. She took me to Lena, Mac's sister. The three of us were the survivors of Birch Haven. Over the last few days, I'd told them what I could about the twelve and what we faced when we escaped. They bore witness to the names of the women who died fighting for their freedom. Cassie. Ellen. Marie. Lara. Majorie. Dana. Shay. My tears fell as I recounted each of their stories, saving Jade for last.

"She's alive," Lena whispered. I knew the words cost her. I knew I'd been lucky. Lena Morris had suffered even worse than Melanie had. I could only imagine the demons she fought just to go on living. "We got Jasmine out."

Then, Eve and Lena told me their secrets. About the network of help the Mammoth Forest wolves had engaged to get those liberated from Birch Haven to safety. Some of them stayed behind, including Lena and Eve. They stayed for Mac. And they stayed because Lena was too fragile to fight anymore.

"Jasmine wanted out of Kentucky," Eve said. "We can get word to her though. If there's something you'd like to tell her about her sister. She knows Jade died. I don't know how. Maybe it's a sister thing, but she always knew."

"Thank you," I said, my heart ached with both sorrow and hope. "I'd like that. I just wish..."

Eve put a hand over mine. "Vera and Melanie," she answered for me. I'd told them their stories too. "You have to have faith. We've put the word out. If any of our people hear anything about either of them, we'll know it. The fact that we haven't is good news. I think your friends made it to wherever they were going."

"I think so too," I said. And I did believe it. We weren't sisters and maybe it was naive, but I believed in my heart that I'd feel it, if anything happened to Vera. "And...they know how to fight."

"There's something else," Eve said, her tone growing solemn. "I didn't want to say anything until I was absolutely sure. But, we got confirmation about an hour ago. It's about your friend, Caroline."

I fell apart. My heart seized and I couldn't breathe. "Oh God. Please." Tears burst from my eyes.

"No!" Eve shouted. She came to me, putting a light hand on my shoulder. "No. Jett, listen to me. She got out. Do you hear me? She's safe. I told you, our network is growing. We have a friend in Clarksville. They arranged for transport. Caroline was life-flighted out of the Clarksville Hospital yesterday. She's at the Cleveland Clinic. Do you hear what I'm saying? She's out. She's going to be okay. She's got a long road ahead of her, but she's going to make it. I promise you."

A sob caught in my throat. I squeezed Eve's hand so hard I was afraid I might hurt her. Lena's expression grew grave. For a moment, she seemed to go someplace else in her head. Gone. Caroline was gone. She got out. The lure of it had to pull on Lena as well.

My joy overflowed and I erupted into a round of hiccupping sobs. "Thank you," I finally managed. "It's everything. It's just...everything." With that, any last shred of doubt I had about Gunnar's family melted away.

I drew in a breath for courage. There was one last secret I had yet to share. In the days since Gunnar brought me here, no one had pressed me. We had all been testing each other, learning to trust. I was Gunnar's, but an outsider. For my part, I'd relied on just myself or Vera for so long, it was hard to let my guard down. So, we waited. We were patient with each other. And yet, with each passing day, I watched Eve's unborn son grow within her. His birth would be cause for celebration, but I knew how much she worried about what was to come.

"I'm ready now," I said, smiling. "Call the others."

Lena slowly rose. I hadn't expected her to leave her rooms. "The rotunda?" she asked.

I shook my head no. "Gunnar said something about a map room. Take me there."

I never would have found it myself. Gunnar's people had it tucked away at the end of a dizzying labyrinth of passageways. It was so small, the shifters couldn't stand fully upright. But, there was a natural ledge in the center of the room. On it, they'd spread a ten-foot topographical map of Kentucky. My heart thundered in my chest. Gunnar came to me. His hand on the small of my back stilled me. He knew how much my next words would cost me, how long I had protected this one last truth.

I let out a breath. Lena stayed behind in her rooms. But, Eve, Molly, Mac, Gunnar, Liam, and now Jagger surrounded the map and waited for me to speak. For Jagger's part, he hung back a little. Like Lena, he was recovering from wounds we couldn't see.

I spread my hands over the map. "I don't know it all," I started, it seemed as good a place as any. "But there is a tunnel system running from here to here." I traced my finger along the Rock-castle River. Gunnar handed me a pencil. I drew in the lines all the way to Camp Hell and beyond.

"We don't know who made them," I said.

Liam cleared his throat. "We have an idea. There was a group of resistance fighters in the early seventies. As far as we know, they're all gone now. You don't think the Pack knows about the tunnels."

"No. They could have caught us easily if they did. The thing is, there are *still* pockets of resistance besides your group. You're just the ones making the most racket right now. And uh...the most organized and powerful. I owe you all my life. This is hard for me. Hard to trust. But, if I don't say these things, I'm afraid you're going to die." I looked at Eve, Molly and Lena. Liam and Mac growled and moved closer to them.

"I'm not saying it to scare you," I continued. "Well, I am. But, the thing is. I've watched you a little bit. Mac, Liam, you're strong. Of course you are. But, you can't be everywhere all the time. The Pack *will* find ways to separate you. And your women don't know how to fight."

"I beg your pardon," Eve said. "My current girth notwithstanding, I've done all right."

"No," I said. "You haven't. If it weren't for your Alphas, you'd be dead already. I'm telling you. You have to do better. You have to know how to defend yourselves against the Pack. If they ever come at you all at once, well, of course there won't be anything you can do. But, that's not usually what they do. Able sends them off one by one. We're human. We're not a big threat, so he doesn't see the need to send a large patrol after any one of us. Plus, I think he has to be more focused when he's directing a group of wolves at once. I don't know, with just a single wolf, he can phone it in a little. If that makes sense. So, he doesn't waste all his energy at one time. One on one, you can defend yourself. I can show you how."

Mac scoffed. "Jett, you're strong. You've survived under incredible odds. But, you're human. You'll never be able to defend yourself against a shifter. Never."

"I've seen her do it," Gunnar said. "Three times. So you might want to shut up and listen."

Jagger pounded his fist against the rock. His eyes blazed gold and even I could feel the pain behind him. He hadn't uttered a word since I met him, but his message was clear. Maybe if his Keara had known what I did, she'd still be alive.

"I don't know if it's always been like this, but the Alpha...Able is old. It's possible it's because he's starting to lose his grip, but we can't be sure of that. One thing I do know is betas are different. I've studied them. I've faced up against them many times. I can train you. But, the betas who Able controls aren't infallible. They have a tell."

"A tell," Molly asked. I didn't know her well yet, but I was already starting to recognize when she wore her clinical hat. A trained veterinarian, Gunnar told me she'd been working the physiological angle for a while.

"They don't think for themselves," I went on. "It's not in their nature to act blindly like Able makes them. That part you know. But, you can *see* it if you know what to look for. I do. It's in their eyes. They fight against it, but Able is too strong. With Alphas like you, it's different. He can't seem to get the same grip on them. But with the betas, you'll see their wolf eyes dim, turning almost amber. It's only a second, two at the most, but if you're ready for it, it's all the time you need. Just before their eyes turn blood-red, they're paralyzed waiting for Able's command. That's when you strike."

I held my hand out imagining a gun in it. A hollow pit formed in my stomach. Again, I thought about the nine I'd had to leave behind. "Of course, it was a surer bet when I had the right ammunition. The bullets we got a hold of were laced with a neurotoxin that could incapacitate a shifter."

"Where'd you get it?" Molly asked, breathless.

"The shifters who helped us when we escaped from Birch Haven gave it to us. Vera and Melanie have two rifles with the last of our ammo. Even without it though, if you shoot a regular bullet into one of the betas at the right time, I think it'll at least give you the chance to make a run for it. You'll do some damage if you hit the head or the heart. But, it's going to take practice."

Mac, Liam and Gunnar were standing near each other. Mac leaned in and whispered something to Liam. Liam turned and looked at Gunnar.

"What?" I asked. Gunnar's face fell. Whatever secret he had, his expression told me I wasn't going to like it.

"We know a guy," Liam answered.

I reared back in shock. "You *know* a guy?"

A murmur ran through the group. Eve and Molly weren't happy either. Connected to Liam and Mac, they could already tell what their men were plotting. I went to Gunnar and laced my fingers with his.

"A few years ago," he said. "We helped a Michigan shifter get over the border. The patrols were lighter then."

"I remember," I said. "That's when your group started making noise. It got harder for a lot of us."

Liam at least had the decency to look chagrined. He shrugged it off. "It's a long shot. And it'll be dangerous as fuck, but..."

"No." Molly, Eve and I said it at the same time. We knew what our men were thinking.

"You can't," I said. "*You* can't! You'll never get over the border. You don't even know if this *guy* is still out there."

"We have friends in Michigan," Mac said. "Or at least, we might. One of them owes us. He'd be dead if we didn't help. Anyway, I think he knows about the ammo you had. Because...well...we saw them shoot some shifters. They went down faster than they should have. I'd always kind of wondered about it, but now with what you're saying, I think it's worth exploring. We need to know at least."

I couldn't believe what I was hearing. They were talking about a suicide mission. A strangled cry escaped from Eve as Mac said, "We have to try."

"No." A deep voice reverberated behind me. Another Alpha, huge as the others, walked into the map room. Shirtless, his powerful muscles were laced with scars just like Jagger. He had a fierce expression, and green eyes that flashed emerald as his inner wolf raged.

"Payne," Molly gasped. She went to him, smoothing her hands over his chest looking for wounds.

Liam, Mac and Gunnar closed ranks around him. He'd been listening to everything. Hard determination lit behind his eyes.

"I'll go," he said. "It has to be me."

Payne walked over to me. He held his hand out for me to shake it. The gesture seemed almost out of place for so feral a man.

Alarm raced through me. I pushed it back and took his hand. It was rough and calloused and his eyes stayed hard.

"Payne," Gunnar said, standing behind me. "This is Jett. She's...mine."

The hint of a smile played at the corner of Payne's mouth. He chewed on a small twig. It was almost as if he needed it to stay connected to the woods above us.

Payne leaned down and kissed my cheek, his rough stubble scraping my jaw. "Thank you," he said. "I've heard a lot about you. Mostly that you saved our boy's ass."

"I uh..."

"Come on," Gunnar said. "You've given them a lot to talk about. Let me know what you decide," he said over my head to Liam and Mac. Jagger had disappeared again without any of us seeing it.

I worried for him, like Molly did. But, something else washed over me that day. It would be hard. It might be impossible. But, these Mammoth Forest wolves had a will to fight and smart women who loved them working by their sides. It was dangerous to hope, but maybe they might just win.

EPILOGUE

JETT
TWO WEEKS LATER...

It had been nearly impossible. In the two weeks since our meeting in the map room, Gunnar and I had scarcely a minute alone. Now that I'd said my piece, the women were eager to learn. Mac found some space topside close to the cave entrance where we could train. In Eve's condition, she could mostly just watch, but I sensed she'd learn quickly once the baby came.

Molly and some of the other women helping Mammoth Forest wolves came ready to train. I worked them hard and their skills at self-defense were slowly improving. Still, we had a long road to go.

Payne kept his word and readied himself to leave. Gunnar wouldn't tell me exactly where he was going. Though he didn't say it, I knew he figured it was for my own protection. Molly said it was better if our Alphas kept some things compartmentalized. I couldn't argue the point.

"Come here," Gunnar said. We'd stolen away to the river that ran alongside the caves. I still marveled that close by, hundreds of tourists walked through the same woods and caves, never knowing what lay just a few hundred yards beneath their feet. My heart pulsed with need as he drew me close. I was hot, sticky and sweaty from a two-hour training session with Molly. Lena had yet to join us. Mac and Molly were worried about her. She'd become more withdrawn each day, not leaving her suite of caves. She'd only let Eve and Mac in to see her.

Gunnar shed his clothes. I watched him in profile, his muscles rippling as he sluiced water over his body. I could watch him like this for hours. Naked. Magnificent. Mine.

"Come here," he said, his eyes lighting with lust. "Let me take care of you." I slid off my jeans and pulled my shirt over my head, tossing it aside.

The water was cooler than I expected. I'd gotten so used to the hot springs down in the caves. I squealed in shock as I sank beneath the rushing waves. It felt good though. I tilted my head back and got my hair wet.

When I felt clean, I went to Gunnar. He'd spread a blanket on the ground. The humid summer air hit my skin as I slipped beside him.

"You're beautiful," he said, lifting a wet lock of hair from my forehead.

"I'm a drowned rat," I answered.

Laughing, he leaned in for a kiss. My nipples pebbled as his naked chest touched mine. Gunnar noticed and reached down to suckle each one. Groaning, I threw my head back.

"I want you," I whispered. "I'll always want you like this, I think."

"I sure hope so," he growled. Wasting no time. He slid his hands beneath my hips and lifted me. In one fluid movement, he set me gently down, straddling him. I bit my lip as my need built to a fever pitch. Gunnar was already huge and hard. I sank down, loving the way he stretched me as his cock slipped inside of me.

"Baby," I gasped as he rooted himself within me. He held my hands, fingers laced together as I arched my back.

"Be still," he said. "Just for a minute. Let me look at you."

I can't imagine what he saw. As always, he turned me into a wild, lustful thing. My nipples turned the color of wine. Goose-bumps covered my flesh. I gripped his hands hard against the urge to thrust. My walls quivered around him as my juices started to flow.

"Gunnar!" I gasped.

"Shh," he said. "You can do it. Just be still."

My body did as he commanded. My Alpha. Always. The mark at the base of my neck throbbed in time with my sex.

"Jett," he whispered. "Sweet Jett. You know, you never told me if that was your real name. Have you always been Jett?"

"J-Janet," I said, my voice hoarse with lust. "I couldn't s-say it when I was little."

His soft laughter threatened to unseat me. "Janet," he repeated. "It's beautiful too. But Jett suits you better."

He leaned forward to catch my bottom lip between his teeth. I groaned with pleasure as his cock moved inside of me. "Gunnar, please."

"Like that," he said. "Always like that. I love when you beg."

"Please!" I shouted, scaring the birds from the trees.

"Mine," he whispered. "Are you mine?"

"Always. Yes."

"I'm yours," he answered. Then, Gunnar leaned back and slid his hands behind his head. Oh, my Alpha meant to enjoy the show.

I couldn't hold back a single second longer. I arched my back and thrust my hips forward, picking up the slow, building rhythm my body called out for. Gunnar grew even harder within me. My body fit his perfectly. We were born for this. Born for each other. How had I ever held back?

I didn't know. I gave in to every sensation. Gunnar's strong heartbeat drove mine. His blood heated my own. I felt his desire as mine crested. We were joined, heart, mind, body, soul. Fated mates. My love.

I cried out his name. The wind carried it as Gunnar put his hands on my hips, holding me steady. My orgasm came, fierce, powerful, primal. I felt it all the way to my toes. It was as if lightning burst from my fingertips. I poured my need into him. Gunnar held steady, letting me drive myself home.

With the last shuddering wave went through me, Gunnar sensed it. Carefully, he turned, holding me in place. He hovered over me, bracing himself on his elbows as I spread my legs even wider. Gunnar drove deep and hard, lustful grace guiding his thrusts. I loved the way his biceps flexed and his chest rippled as he drove himself ever deeper. Then, he let go. We soared. Gunnar filled me with heat and light as I wrapped my legs around his waist and took everything he could give.

He whispered my name against my temple as he finally came back down. Curling himself around me, we watched the stars come out.

Later, he turned to me. "Do I make you happy?" he asked.

I kissed him. "Of course you do."

"If the day ever came that I asked you to do something for me, would you?"

His expression grew serious. The stars lit his eyes. "Gunnar..."

"You know how to take care of yourself," he said, bringing my palm to his lips. "Someday, you may have to....without me."

"Don't," I said. "It's bad luck. There's no need."

But, I knew my Alpha well. I'd seen the urge burning through him. He had the kill in his sights. In his heart, he believed he could bring Able Valent down.

"I love you," I said.

Gunnar pulled me to him. "Jett..."

"I *love* you," I said. "So don't ask the thing you think you have to. I'm where I want to be."

"But, I could do it. We have the means. I could help you find Jasmine and the others who got out of Birch Haven. You could go north. You could get away from the Pack forever. So when the time comes...when I have to do what you *know* I have to do, I know you'll be safe."

I kissed him. "And you know it doesn't work that way. We're fated, remember? My place is with you. And *when* and if that time comes, I'll be here to help you in whatever way I can. You may be an Alpha, but you know you can't win this alone. You're stuck with me, buddy. I've already made that choice."

I felt relief flood through him. Had he really had any doubt? I held him close as I always would.

"I love you too," he whispered. "God help us both, but I do."

"I know," I said, laughing. "Remember, you can't hide from me here anymore." I pointed to his forehead. "Or here." I pointed to his heart. "Or here," I said, laughing as I slid my hand along his inner thigh.

"Mmmm," he answered, already growing hard again. "You're the most incredible woman I've ever known."

"Yes," I smiled. "Maybe I am. But promise me, whatever comes, you'll face it *with* me. Neither of us will do this alone."

He let out a breath he'd been holding, then kissed me once again. "Promise," he finally said.

I settled against him as the moon rose high and bright. It's an incredible thing, sharing a heart. The bond between my Alpha and me grew ever stronger. I knew there were tougher battles to come. I knew not everyone we loved might survive it. But, I knew the bond between Gunnar and me would never break.

Another truth thundered through me, becoming just as real and solid as the pulse we now shared. Gunnar's eyes glinted with the same knowledge as he locked his gaze with mine. Someday, somehow, we knew we would win.

THE END

A NOTE FROM KIMBER WHITE

For a first look at my next new release, sign up for my newsletter today. You'll be the first to know about my new releases and special discounts available only to subscribers. You'll also get a FREE EBOOK right now, as a special welcome gift for joining. I promise not to spam you, share your email or engage in other general assholery. You can unsubscribe anytime you like (I'll only cry a little). You can sign up here! http://www.kimber-white.com/newsletter-signup

Psst . . . can I ask you a favor?

If you liked this story, can you do something for me? Please consider leaving a review. Reviews help authors like me stay visible and allow me to keep bringing you more stories. Reviews are the fuel that keeps us going. Please and thank you.

And if you STILL want more, I'd love to hang out with you on Facebook. I like to share story ideas, casting pics, and general insanity on a regular basis.

From the bottom of my heart though, THANK YOU for your support. You rock hard.

See you on the wild side!

Kimber

KimberWhite.com

kimberwhiteauthor@gmail.com

BOOKS BY KIMBER WHITE

Mammoth Forest Wolves

Liam

Mac

Gunnar

Payne

Jagger

Wild Ridge Bears Series

Lord of the Bears (featuring Jaxson)

Outlaw of the Bears (featuring Cullen)

Rebel of the Bears (featuring Simon)

Curse of the Bears (Featuring Rafe)

Last of the Bears (Featuring Bo and Trevor)

Wild Lake Wolves Series

Rogue Alpha

Dark Wolf

Primal Heat

Savage Moon

Hunter's Heart

Wild Lake Wolves Prequel Novels

Wild Hearts

Stolen Mate

Claimed by the Pack (Wolf Shifter Series)

The Alpha's Mark

Sweet Submission

Rising Heat

Pack Wars

30330254R00170

Made in the USA
Lexington, KY
08 February 2019